D0356867

L. RIFKIN
THE NINE LIVES OF
RomeoCrumb

LIFE FOUR

Illustrations by Kurt Hartman

Stratford Road
Press, Ltd.

This is a work of fiction. Any resemblance to actual persons, living or dead, animals, business, events, or locales is entirely coincidental.

Library of Congress Control Number: 2007942166

ISBN: 978-0-9743221-9-3

Designed by Sean Murphy
www.seanmurphydesigns.com
and
Kurt Hartman
www.kurthartman.com

Printed in the United States of America.

LIFE FOUR

Chapter One

It took two long years to finish the repairs before the Factory was finally ready to officially reopen. Everyone was thrilled. Not having a safe common ground was becoming increasingly difficult. Initially, the death of Fidel, leader of the Alleys, and the Sticks's greatest enemy, was cause for some celebration, but soon things began to dwindle. Friends saw less of each other. Classes were to a bare minimum, but now that would all come to an end.

The damage caused during the Vent City revolt was far more extensive than the Sticks had originally believed. Aside from the cosmetic problems, much of the old building was in need of major reconstruction. Doors needed to be replaced, the elevator needed to be rebuilt, and somebody needed to take care of that pungent, lingering smell the Alleys left behind before the dogs ran them out. Because of their size and limited supply of equipment, it took the Sticks a full two years to finish all this, as well as countless other minor jobs. During that long, arduous time, several organized events still managed to be carried on without much disruption. Random outdoor social functions and classroom activities helped to strengthen the lagging Stick spirit as the Factory slowly grew from its dusty shambles.

The city was getting its own makeover too. Excitement filled the air. In just two days the first annual city marathon was set to take place. The fastest and fittest runners would spill down the 26.2 mile course through the many winding streets, around the park, along the river, hoping to regain their own sense of community and vigor. Sponsorships benefited the city's economy adding a little glimmer of hope to the depressed standard of life everyone felt. The winner of the race would receive an all expense paid trip to the west coast, something everyone dreamed of. A peek at the good life.

"Romeo, have you written your speech for the Factory's big reopening ceremony?" Tabitha asked, a splotchy painting smock tied around her

Life Four

middle. "I bet you'll say something really great. What an event it's gonna be!" With a firm stroke of her brush, she continued covering a rotted beam with bright blue paint.

Sulking in an old, hollow carpet tube, Romeo drummed his claws against the cardboard and rolled his eyes. "Speech? Speech?" he echoed from the inside. "Are you nuts? I'm not giving no stupid speech! No way!"

Tabitha remained calm. "Sure you are," she reminded him. "Remember, you agreed to it during the planning. I heard you."

"Look, that was a long time ago. Things have changed. I could care less about some dumb ceremony," Romeo snapped as he angrily wiggled deeper into the tube.

"Oh, don't be a sour puss. Come on, Romeo," Tabitha teased. "You know you're going to write that speech no matter how much you protest." She tried to humor him out of his enduring funk once again, but to no avail. Finally, she just gave up.

But Romeo was right, things had changed. Most importantly, his dire predictions about Dennis were correct. He was out of Romeo's life forever. Gone. Snap. Just like that. Getting the sleepy potion made it impossible for Romeo to ever return home. Dennis thought he was dead from the poisonous liquid the Vet injected into his vein. To a human, dead meant dead. The poor boy was heartsick at the death of his beloved cat, and Romeo had no choice but to play along. Since

Chapter One

awakening from death number three, Romeo had been left with an empty hole in the pit of his stomach. He felt everyone he ever loved had been unfairly snatched away. Everything he dreamed of, gone. It was now two long years since his veterinary demise, and what remained of the once likable young Romeo was a heated, angry grouch. He had grown into the kind of teenager no one wanted to be around. No one, that is, except Candle. She followed him like a shadow.

While Romeo lay around the musty Factory not lifting a paw, the rest of the Factory Sticks proudly embraced their accomplishments in rebuilding their home away from home. Most of all, they enjoyed the peace they had earned. With Fidel, their most hated rival dead, the past two years had been like a vacation. Without his power dripping over them, life's challenges were faced head-on, and life itself was more appreciated than ever. Nothing was perfect, of course. Caution remained at high alert. The evil dogs were still out there, and the Pound van continued its deadly rounds looking for strays. Of course, the Sticks were still keenly aware of the rest of the Alleys, some more angry and hostile than ever. Though they always posed a potential threat to the Sticks, without their maniacal leader, Fidel, they seemed less menacing. The Sticks let a newfound confidence seep into their little feline bodies, reaching every pore, pulsing through their veins. When they walked the city streets, they held their heads proudly, noses to the air, paws firmly planted on the ground. Over time, they began to spend more of their days outside, playing and keeping fit in the very wind and air the Alleys so often had stolen from them. Nothing could stop them now.

Despite the upcoming marathon, the city continued to suffer with little financial recovery for its citizens. As suspected, Mayor Hashback had proven a poor choice to lead them out of the depression. He had spent much of his narcissistic reign sopping up their hopes and dreams with his greedy, sponge-like ways. After he was unofficially accused of being involved in former Mayor Crowman's murder, things seemed even more hopeless, but with no hard evidence, just heavy suspicion, Hashback was allowed to continue his term. However, he devoted much precious time to defending himself and not to governing. None of the citizens or animals for that matter had any cause to doubt his guilt. Thus, a cold, cruel cloud still hung over the city like a chocking smog, at least until the next election.

But in spite of the hard times, hope grew in the most unlikely of places. These difficult years brought families together in spirit, building a new inner strength and vitality. Seeing this togetherness happening around him was perhaps what made Romeo all the more sad and rebellious. He had no family anymore. Dennis and his parents were out of his life forever. He imagined himself completely

Chapter One

forgotten by the Crumb clan. Pierre, the poodle, was now Dennis's best pal. Romeo pictured them playing together, just like he used to do. Even though Romeo had realized the dream of having his own birth father back, it simply wasn't enough. Without Dennis, Romeo no longer felt a sense of belonging, something he missed more than he could have ever imagined. He was a Stick, and Sticks had homes and people who loved them. Fidel and his wicked reign of terror had taken all that away from him.

While Tabitha playfully spread the pretty blue paint over the beam to cover up the nasty Alley graffiti, Romeo watched from inside the cardboard tube. "What do you think, Romeo?" she asked staring proudly at her blue swirls. "Doesn't that look better than those foul words?"

"Who cares," Romeo mumbled.

Tabitha stuck her nose in the tube and reached for him with her wet brush. "Aw, come on, Romeo," she prodded. "You didn't even look. Why don't you come out of there and..."

"Shut up and leave me alone!" Romeo hollered, dashing out the other end.

Tabitha watched Romeo run away in an angry huff, her brush dripping gobs of gooey paint onto the floor.

As Romeo dashed through the rec room, he knocked headfirst into Mr. Sox, still the oldest and wisest Stick around. Mr. Sox toppled to the cold floor, his glasses crumbling beneath him.

Life Four

"Whoa, Romeo!" he cried. "Watch where you're going, son." With little, slow movements, Mr. Sox brushed himself off and struggled to get up. "Will you help me, son?" he asked Romeo who stood motionless to the side.

Romeo reached out one paw too far away for Mr. Sox to grab. "Come on, I haven't got all day," he grumbled.

Frustrated and angry, Mr. Sox flopped back down to the ground, crushing his wire rims even more. He couldn't reach Romeo's paw, let alone see it without his spectacles. "Just forget it, Romeo! If you can't help me, then..."

"Fine!" Romeo snapped, heading for the door.

Mr. Sox watched Romeo's blurry figure dash out of sight. "Wait! Come back, Romeo!" he called. "I'm sorry I lost my temper! Come over here and we'll talk! You know, like we used to!" Over the past two years Mr. Sox had tried everything. Calmness, he thought, was the best solution to Romeo's flaring temper, though Romeo just scoffed at him. In fact, desperate for some sort of advice, Sox was eagerly anticipating his upcoming appointment with a leading cat therapist.

Mr. Sox twisted his body toward the hallway, a sharp chunk of his glasses pinching his leg.

"Talk? Talk?" Romeo turned and blurted, resentment burning in his eyes. "Are you going to tell me more lies?" In a flash, he was heading back toward the door.

Chapter One

"What lies? What are you talking about?" Mr. Sox thundered, his chest beginning to ache within his frail body.

Romeo turned and gave him a cold stare. "Everything you ever told me was a lie! Why can't everyone just leave me alone?" he screamed, tearing down the long hallway.

"But wait! Don't go outside!" Mr. Sox warned. "There's supposed to be a big storm tonight!" Without his glasses Mr. Sox couldn't see Romeo's shape anymore, nor did he feel the vibrations of his pawsteps. "I'm going to get your father. Maybe he can snap some sense into you!" Sox shouted toward the empty hallway.

But it was too late. Romeo had already crashed through the front entrance and zoomed out into the dark, lonely night.

Mr. Sox was right about one thing. A wicked storm was brewing. Romeo could smell it. A heavy slate of storm clouds rolled over the city for the first time in weeks. Booms of thunder rattled between the buildings. Violent winds viscously pulled at Romeo's body like taffy, tossing him all over the street as the rain started to pelt.

As Romeo fought the howling weather, he saw a street lamp up ahead. Its red, green, and yellow lights flickered on and off in the blurry shadows dissolving together into an eerie purplish glow. Struggling against the fierce gusts, Romeo made his way to the lamppost. Just as he reached out his paw to grab it, a wild sting of wind slapped

Life Four

him to the ground right on his bottom. Crouching low to the concrete, Romeo inched himself up to the street lamp with one final struggle, wrapped his front paws around its metal base and hung on. His head slumped against the pole as a sudden and explosive noise caught his attention.

"What's that?" he shrieked, staring up into the stormy night. Romeo gazed wide eyed as the sky suddenly tore open and a neon bolt of lightening flashed across the city skyline like a fireball. The street lamp began to rattle and quake, and in a blink Romeo was struck by a hot jolt of golden fire. He screamed in agony as the painful volts sizzled through his body. His paws exploded off the pole as he was catapulted ten feet onto the hard sidewalk, his body charred and lifeless. Unconscious but alive, he lay there alone on the soaked pavement, rain ravaging his fur. Above, the hurricane raged on flashing its neon teeth to all in its path.

Chapter Two

Romeo shook his head and opened his eyes. To his amazement he was no longer outside in the violent storm, but had somehow arrived in a strange, dark room. It was cold and damp and cave-like. Still in a state of shock, he quickly moved his paw to rub his eyes, but came to a horrifying discovery. He couldn't lift his arm.

"I'm paralyzed!" he screamed.

True, Romeo couldn't move. But paralyzed? No. He was strapped down tightly to a hard, cold table. Wrapped in crushing leather ropes, he began

Life Four

to wiggle and squirm. He thrust his front paws against the thick straps over and over. Stopping to catch his breath, his suspecting eyes swirled around the quiet, candle lit room, desperate for answers. Where was he?

"Get me outta here! Help!" he hollered from his mysterious clutches. His mind began to go crazy. Just as Romeo opened his mouth to let out another wail, he heard an alarming noise, a noise like nothing he had ever heard before.

"Squeak! Squeak! Squeak!" Squeals like piercing needles to his ears echoed all around him.

"Who's there?" Romeo quivered.

"Squeak! Squeak! Squeak!" The high-pitched screeches grew louder and closer.

And then it hit him like that very bolt of lightning. Romeo realized what the awful sound was. Rats! Dozens of them! Maybe hundreds! His skin crawled as the horrifying sounds surrounded him. From the corner of his eye, he could see long, slithering tails pass underneath the table, gliding effortlessly like water. Spiny claws grazed over his feet and around his ears, tickling his fur and making shrilling noises, enough to break his eardrums. Romeo's heart pounded faster, sweat soaking his forehead.

"Get offa me!" he roared, feeling the weight of their bodies slowly climbing on top of his hind legs. They felt heavy. Then one leaped onto his chest, its nails digging into his fur. It was huge. Three times the size of any normal rat. "Ouch! Get

Chapter Two

off!" Romeo screamed in horror. He was doomed. He knew it. With his eyes shut tight, he could sense the rat's deep, beady eyeballs staring right through him and feel its hot breath scorching his nose. With one final gulp, Romeo waited for its big, sharp, grisly teeth to begin feasting on his flesh. And then...

"Romeo!" someone shrieked in his ears. "Romeo! Open your eyes!"

Romeo found himself staring face to face with a monstrous rat. Its fur was dirt brown and swirling with tiny, white worms. Its long, gritty tongue simmered between jagged, sharp teeth. This was no ordinary rat! It was a Vent City rat!

"Wh..what do you want?" Romeo asked. "What's g..going on?"

"Awe, poor little pussy's scared," the rat teased with a snide grin. It leaned in closer. "You're the one they call Romeo, right?" it sneered. "They call me Hog," the rat boasted. "We've been looking for you."

Romeo turned his head away from the rat's disgusting, foul breath. "Me?" he quivered. "Why would you be looking for me?"

Hog circled Romeo's body as he lay imprisoned by the straps. The rest of the grisly rodents edged their way around the table, one more hideous than the next. "Do you know where you are?" echoed Hog's deep voice.

Romeo shook his head *no* under his confinements.

Life Four

"You're in what's left of Vent City! You remember this place, don't you Romeo?" it asked hauntingly. "The place you destroyed just two short years ago! Surely you can't forget that!"

"What are you talking about? Let me outta here! Now!" Romeo pleaded.

"Not so fast, kid! Not so fast!" Some of the maggots fell off Hog and began to parade around Romeo's belly. "Since you and your sweet daddy took on that heroic deed, things went a little wrong, didn't they? No happy ending, eh?"

"I don't know!" Romeo blared. "I don't know what you're talking about!"

"I think you know exactly what I'm talking about," the rat said slowly, towering right above Romeo's face.

"I don't! I swear!" But Romeo did know what the smelly rodent was getting at. It was something so awful he had chosen to forget it.

"Admit it!" Hog screamed in a coughing fit, staring down at Romeo with his almost sightless eyes, clouded whitish-gray with pinpoint pupils from years of living in darkness. They were disgusting. Romeo tried to look away. "You know what happened!"

"Don't!"

"Do!"

"Don't!" Romeo yelled.

"Do!"

"All right! All right!" Romeo cried, broken by the moment, maggots squirming all around

Chapter Two

him. "They're gone! All right! Happy now?" Romeo tried to hide his head deeply into the table as he wept the shame from his eyes.

"So you admit it!" Hog squealed with one fist high above him. "Very good, Romeo." The rat continued with a calm intimidation. "Very good, boy. Let's review and you'll see, you'll feel better once you've faced the truth."

"No! No! I can't! Please don't say it!" Romeo begged. "It was too awful! I don't want to hear it!"

"Now, now, don't be such a wuss," Hog chided. "Let's back up. I helped the Sticks fight the big, mean Alley cats. Sound familiar? Hmmm?"

Romeo moaned and twisted.

"Good. Now, after that fun victory celebration, remind me again what happened to all your newly freed mutant friends. What fate awaited them?" Hog teased, petting another rat on the tail.

"They left," Romeo mumbled. His paws were clenched and his jaw tight.

"A little louder please."

"They ran away! Went into hiding again!" Romeo thundered, pain in his voice.

"Yes, now I remember," the rat said teasingly. "You convinced the Vent City mutants that they would be normal animals and become part of the real city again. But the city didn't like them, did they? They didn't accept those poor, disgusting creatures back into their world, am I right?" he said dramatically waving his massive paws above his head. "They laughed at them! Pointed and stared! Isn't that so, Romeo? They were feared and loathed by the people, and life was unbearable for the pathetic, misled misfits!"

"Yes! It's true!" Romeo exploded. "They were too ugly! As ugly as you! People were scared! The mayor was going to have them killed! They had to get out of the city! It was my fault! They're gone! Every one of them! I didn't think it would end that way! You gotta believe me! I just wanted them to breathe fresh, clean air once again!" Romeo then took in a quick breath and tried desperately to control his anger. "But what do you care? You rats hated the mutants!" He paused for a second then spit out the words he feared had an answer. "What do you really want from me?"

"What do I want from you?" Hog repeated. "Good question. Let me tell you, Romeo!"

Suddenly, one of the other rats began to tickle Romeo's back paw. "Look, Hog," it cackled. "The kitty's ticklish."

Hog swatted the pesky rat out of the way. "Me and my family of rats relied on those mutants! They provided us with food down here! Since they've been gone, we've had next to nothing to eat! My family is hungry! Look at them! They're skinny and drawn!" he blared, pointing to his colony. He was right. Their once flabby bellies were limp and crinkled. Their ribs bulged under their skin like tumors. "Do you know what happens when rats get hungry?" Hog asked menacingly.

Chapter Two

"I th..thought the mutants didn't like you," Romeo cried with confusion. "I thought they were afraid of you. Why would they give you food?" He looked dazed at the other rats as they nibbled on the maggots embedded in their fur.

"Silly, silly, Romeo," Hog teased. "They didn't give us food. We took theirs!" Hog leaned in real close to Romeo's ear and whispered. "In fact, we even had a bite of them now and again while they were sleeping, of course. Some were very tasty."

"Gross!" Romeo grimaced. "You bit into them? You're sick!"

Hog looked at him with his beady eyes. "At least we don't eat rats like you do!" he wheezed with malicious revenge.

"Yeah!" the others agreed.

"I don't understand!" Romeo said, thinking quickly. "Why don't you eat the thrown away junk food at the train station like the mice do? There's plenty to go around up there!"

"We're tired of candy wrappers and empty soda cans! The time has come for something better!" Hog drooled. "It's hard for us to see up there. We don't have much sight left after living for years without light. Many rats are completely blind. Besides, it's not easy running up all those stairs every time we want to eat. Not very pleasant, is it?" Hog snapped.

"I still don't know what any of this has to do with me!" Romeo cried. "Why won't you let me go?"

Life Four

"Let me get right to the point," Hog said in a low, heavy voice, still planted firmly on Romeo's beating chest. "We miss the full supply of treats we had right here in Vent City that the mutants provided. Since they're all gone, thanks to you, we're starving to death down here!" he paused for a breath. "Now listen closely, this is where you come in. After all, you owe us. You're the one who caused this mess, Mr. Hero!"

"I can't do anything!" Romeo whined.

"Well, you may want to rethink that. We've elected you to deliver us our daily supply of food," Hog said in a low murmur, drumming his claws on Romeo's stomach. "It was our good fortune that the lightning bolt knocked you out. We've tried to catnap you before," he said sneakily.

"Get you food?" Romeo cried. "That's impossible! You've got dozens of rats..."

"Let me put it this way. You get us food or Dennis will die!" Hog roared.

"What?" Romeo cried, taking in a deep breath of rat fumes. "Dennis? What does he have to do with this? How do you know about Dennis anyway? You're lying!"

"Does this look like a lie?" Hog lifted an old photo of Dennis and Romeo high over his head. It was the black and white one Dennis kept on his nightstand.

"How'd you get that?" Romeo wailed in disbelief.

Hog whacked his tail hard against Romeo's

Chapter Two

side. Romeo let out a piercing cry. "I need to make sure you live up to your end of the bargain, that's all," Hog explained with evil intentions.

"What bargain? What are you talking about?"

"It's simple, really," Hog said patronizingly. "You are going to bring us the goods. A lot to start."

"No way! Not a chance!" Romeo hollered. "That's impossible!"

"Then it's lights out for Dennis!" Hog teased, slowly tearing the photograph in half.

Romeo closed his eyes and counted to ten. The image in the photo flickered in his brain. Mr. Crumb snapped it the day Romeo arrived. He was just a kitten. It was Dennis's favorite picture. They were so happy then.

Romeo thought hard. Perhaps Hog was only bluffing. After all, how much damage could a practically blind rat do to a human boy like Dennis? Deciding he couldn't risk the consequences, Romeo made up his mind. He had no other choice. "All right," he said calmly. "I'll do it. " He stared up at Hog and swallowed hard. "Tell me what you want me to do."

Hog glared at him with a wide grin. "At precisely seven A.M. the catering table for the city marathon will be open for members of the press. There will be all sorts of yummy meats, cheeses, crackers, loads of stuff." Beads of drool dripped from his mouth. "You'll bring all that food down to Vent City, but don't wait till seven or you'll miss your chance. The table will be swamped with reporters by then. Go early, and don't screw up! Then maybe, just maybe, if you do a good job I'll save a piece of cheese for you. Just one, of course." Hog licked the drool from his mouth and continued. "You have thirty-six hours to complete your first assignment. We're very hungry, and the more hungry we get the meaner we get, so hop to it! I suggest you start formulating your plan as soon as possible."

"Are you crazy?" Romeo yelled. "I can't bring a whole table of food down here! How about just a few sandwiches or some bread..."

"Thirty-six hours," Hog repeated as he slowly scurried into the darkness and disappeared. As Romeo allowed the idea of this horrible task to sink in, he began to hear gritty little noises all around him. From the corner of his eye he saw several rats gnawing at the leather ropes. One of them spoke softly in his ear.

"You're at the first corner out of four." The rat spoke quickly with leather between his teeth, almost as if he cared. "Go to the second corner east of here at the station near the old, abandoned school house. You can't miss it. It's a doozy. You'll meet Trixie. She can help, as long as she likes you. You can't do this alone. I'm awfully hungry." With that, the rats had savagely torn the ropes apart.

"What?" Romeo cried confused.

"Go quick!" another rat advised. "You don't have much time. Hog always keeps his word.

Chapter Two

Life Four

Always. Just get us the food, and Dennis will be all right. If you fail, Hog promises us a juicy meal of raw boy," he cackled and coughed.

"Remember, find Trixie! It's your best bet," the first rat affirmed. He wanted that food fast. "Tell her you're helping Hog. She likes Hog."

Just then, the final rope detached from Romeo's leg. As he was about to make a quick escape, he suddenly felt a scratchy cloth slip over his head. "What's going on?" he wailed. A few seconds of silence, then whack! Romeo was hit hard by a heavy object. He passed out cold.

Romeo awoke in an old, ratty potato sack under the very street lamp he had clung to during the storm.

Though the rain had stopped, the huge, swelling bump on Romeo's head felt worse than that sizzling jolt of lightning. By some miracle, he had survived both.

What a dream, he pondered poking his head out of the sack. Romeo looked down. Many claw prints dotted the mud surrounding him heading back to the station. *Rat prints!* Romeo said to himself. *It wasn't a dream. They were here.*

Chapter Three

After Romeo left, Hog held an emergency meeting with his top rats. "Listen up, gentlemen," he began, nibbling on an old toothpaste tube. "Good work today. That little nobody's scared silly. Sucker," he chuckled as the sounds of his grumbling tummy vibrated the ground below. "We've got him wrapped around our claws."

"You said it," another rat agreed. "He's a stupid one! He'll be back with food. I know it."

"I'm sending the three of you out there to keep an eye on him, just like we planned," Hog went on with his mysterious eyes, pointing to his three henchrats. "Make sure he's not eating our grub, not one morsel! Watch him like a hawk, but don't let him see you. He'll wonder why you're not getting the goods yourselves. Check on that Dennis too. We don't want any trouble with him."

"He don't know nothing," one of the rats said.

Hog began to sizzle. "Just make sure."

"What if Romeo can't do it?" another asked. "I mean, I don't see how he can carry all that food down here."

"Then we'll bring him and that stupid boy to the fourth corner! Romeo will get what he really deserves!" Hog said maniacally. "Then we'll have the real fun!" Hog punched a hole right through the toothpaste tube. "You like roast cat, don't you?" The rats looked at each other with wicked grins.

Romeo looked up into the night. The thunderous clouds were passing. The storm had ended. His eyes immediately went to the rusted, round clock that seemed to grow out of the subway station roof. It hung like an old moon over the double doors. Its large, pointy black hands wiggled and shook from the vibrations of the chiming bells.

Eight o'clock, he noted, quickly calculating in his head. Thirty-five hours. How am I going to pull this off? Romeo lifted himself up and began to hobble back to the Factory. His skin was hot, though he was wet and soggy. Patches of his grey and black fur had been zapped off or singed by the

Chapter Three

lightning, and his left ear rang like the dickens.

He trotted on through the low, evening fog, ignoring the familiar eerie moans pouring from the lonely alleyways. For once, he had bigger problems than worrying about what the Alleys might do if they spotted him.

Back at the Factory, Romeo knocked the working crew out of his way and bolted inside. "What's the big idea?" Waffles snapped, bottoms up in a tub of wet cement.

"Sorry man," Romeo cried, not even looking back to see what he had done.

Waffles wiggled himself from the gooey glue and rubbed his eyes clean. "That Romeo," he grumbled. "I've had just about enough of him and his attitude." Waffles violently shook the remaining cement drops from his fur.

"Me too," Vittles agreed, dodging the flying debris. Both of them peeked into the hallway, shooting Romeo a nasty glare.

"What happened to you?" Candle asked, noticing a thin layer of steam hovering over Romeo's body as he ran into the rec room. Since the Vent City revolt, she had been accepted into the Stick community per Romeo's request. At first he seemed to like this wayward little Alley girl. After their victory, they had begun a new friendship, instantly bonding. But as time passed, things began to change. As Romeo sunk deeper into his adolescent depression, he hardly gave her a second glance. He was all mixed up. She didn't understand why. "Romeo?" Candle cried again. "What happened to you?"

Romeo walked in tight circles around the new rec room, seemingly preoccupied and disoriented. Everyone around him was still preparing for the Factory's opening ceremony. As usual, Romeo played no part, circling nervously. Candle dashed up to him again. "Do you mind?" Romeo snapped. "I'm trying to walk here!"

"I just want to help," she said. "Why don't you give me a chance?"

"Why don't you leave me alone?" Romeo hollered. "Go back to your strings!" Candle loved string, always had. Romeo ran through the room and bolted out the front door. Candle watched him disappear.

As Romeo pounded up the street, his mind raced with thoughts of Hog and the rats. Go to the second corner? Was it safe? He'd heard of the four corners from his teachers. Like Vent City itself, the four corners were feared and forbidden places, full of mystery, danger, and suspense. At the four farthest edges of the city, they existed like four black holes somewhere under the streets. Supposedly, no one ever came out alive. Well, at least that was untrue, because Romeo had already been to the first and farthest west corner and lived to tell about it. But rumor said that it was supposedly the least threatening corner of the four.

While Romeo raced on, Bait sat in a far away alley licking the crud off a dented tin can.

Chapter Three

"Gimme some o' that!" Cheeseburger howled, smelling the delicious molded cheese. "I'm hungry!"

Bait quickly turned away from his meaty friend, clutching the tasty can tightly in his grubby paws. "Get your own dinner!" he cracked. "Dis is mine!"

Bait chipped off the last crusty spot of the potato cheese soup and savagely tossed the can right at Cheeseburger's head. "Hey, what's the big idea?"

"Dat's funny! I wanna do that again!" Bait laughed, reaching for another can. With it firmly in his paw, he stuck out his tongue and prepared his throw. He wound his arm in large circles, his beady eyes aiming right for Cheeseburger's snout. The can went sailing through the mist like a rocket. Cheeseburger ducked his head under his paws, when out of nowhere the hazy image of a cat crept in the alleyway. Its shadow slowly edged up the brick wall. The can sailed forward, missing Cheeseburger completely and hitting the mystery cat with a wallop. The cat crashed to the ground with a loud thud. Bait stood motionless. Cheeseburger hadn't seen anything. His eyes were tightly shut.

"Oh, just throw it and get it over with!" Cheeseburger whined.

"Get up, dummy!" Bait yelled. "I hit somebody! I hit somebody!"

"Huh?" Cheeseburger asked, his eyes

peeking over his paws.

Bait raced up to his victim. It was a cat all right, and it was out cold. Dead, actually.

"Bait! Ya killed him!" Cheeseburger cried. With all his mighty strength, Bait reached for its feet and began dragging him deeper into the alley. "Help me, wouldya?" he called to Cheeseburger.

Cheeseburger leapt up. "Uh, shouldn't we get somebody?" he asked. "Don't you think we should get some help. I mean, what if he's a..."

"Look, so long as Fidel's not around, I'm in charge of us Alleys, see," Bait reminded with his meek, whiny voice. "I says we take a closer look."

They managed to drag the cat all the way to the rear of the alley. Its golden fur was dripping wet and slick from a fine layer of expensive fur gel. It wore a brown vest, nicely fitted around its middle, and pretty, silk pants...paisley. Beside him was a suspicious looking leather pocketbook, stolen from an old woman no doubt. Around his neck was a fancy collar, the kind only the richest Sticks wore. The tag read *Irving*.

"What's it say?" Cheeseburger asked, staring down at the shiny metal.

"How am I supposed to know?" Bait whined.

Bait walked suspiciously around the cat just like Fidel would have done. "Ouch!" he howled. "I stepped on a rock!" So much for being a tough guy.

"What are we gonna do?" Cheeseburger asked. "What if he wants to kill us? I'm too young to die again! Papa! Help me! Help!"

Bait noticed the old, leather bag. He began to panic. "Maybe he's got something real sharp in dat bag there!" Bait exploded. "What if he's gonna slice us up like fishies? You know, like in those Japanese restaurants."

They ran in horror to the other side of the alley, clinging onto each other for dear life. After a long while, the mystery cat began to twitch. His whiskers flopped up and down, and his vest buttons popped open. Slowly and steadily, he came back to life.

"Where...am I?" he mumbled, his head throbbing. "My, my, what happened?"

"Stand back, Stick!" Bait growled in a pathetic attempt at a karate pose. "I'll knock ya out again!" He leapt up to the rim of a garbage can full of banana peels, slicing his paws through the air. He almost pulled it off until he lost his balance and fell to the bottom.

"Charge!" Cheeseburger hollered, bolting forward like a cannonball eager to save the day. His big, pudgy body careened forward, his head low to the ground. Irving ducked out of the way just in the nick of time, sending Cheeseburger headfirst into Bait's can knocking it and the banana peels to the ground.

"Get offa me!" Bait screamed, a rotted peel dangling from his nose.

Cheeseburger flicked it off and laughed.

As Bait and Cheeseburger swirled around

in the gooey mess, Irving carefully approached. "Excuse me, gentlemen," he said with a hint of hoity-toityness. "Pardon me, but I was wondering if you could point me in the right direction." He looked at the two jostling cats and stood up tall, re-styling the gelled fur atop his wet head and re-buttontening his vest.

Bait's wicked scowl emerged from under the banana sludge. "What'ya want, Fancy Pants?" Bait teased.

"Ha! Dat's a good one," echoed Cheeseburger's voice from the depths of the pile.

Irving snatched up his pocketbook as if it were his very important briefcase. He straightened his vest and ran his tongue along his fine teeth. "I said, I was wondering if you males could point me in the right direction," he explained. "You see ol' chaps, I just arrived from out of town and I'm looking for a good flat and some respectable work. Have you any advice?"

Bait and Cheeseburger looked at each other, still covered in banana goop. Unable to contain themselves, they exploded into a ruckus laughter.

"Get a loada him!" Bait roared.

"You got that right, old chap!" Cheeseburger cackled.

Irving glared at them, clutching his dearly beloved pocketbook. He cleared his throat again. "I said, do you know of any flats? My paws are dreadfully tired, and I'd rather not walk much further."

"How dreadful," Bait howled dramatically.

"Very well, then," Irving finally said. He turned around to leave when...

"Listen up, Stick!" Bait cracked, suddenly bubbling with anger. "Don't ya know who you're talking to? Whadaya think you're doin' here anyways? Aren't you late for tea or something?"

"Ha! Dat's a good one too, Bait," Cheeseburger cried.

Irving took a conservative step back and slowly blinked his eyes. "Listen, gentlemales, I'm sorry for the misunderstanding but I can assure you, I am not a Stick, whatever that is!"

"Then what's with da collar?" Cheeseburger asked, nose to the air.

Irving looked down and found his expensive tag. "Oh, this," he said. "You see, back home I was in a...bit of trouble. Yes, that's it, trouble. A dear friend of mine fashioned this safety collar for me. He was quite good at that sort of thing. Anyway, I hopped on a large steamer bringing only with me what you see here. A fine fellow on board told me to seek out the Alley cats. He said they may be able to help me find work."

"Whadaya tink, Bait?" Cheeseburger whispered. "What would Fidel do with 'im?"

"I don't know! I don't know! Let me think!" Bait answered, gnawing on his claws like a little boy. Thinking was a concept Bait hadn't quite been able to grasp yet. Maybe in the next life.

Life Four

"All right," he finally said, "you can stay here and work for us." Cheeseburger shot him a look and slugged him in the arm. Bait whacked him back with his tail. "You sure you're no Stick?"

"Positive." Irving looked around at the drab alleyway. It was littered with garbage and laced in a thick layer of filth. "So, I would live here?" he asked with a frown. "In this...place?"

"Sure. Why not? Something wrong wit it?" Cheeseburger snapped, trying to act tough. He puffed out his chest and leaned forward when a sudden and overpowering belch erupted from his mouth. "Sorry."

"Okay, I suppose I could stay here for a bit," Irving reluctantly agreed. "But I need to tidy up before bedtime. Do you mind?"

"Be my guest," Bait said. "Take dat spot over der," Bait pointed, directing him to the far corner. "Stay there for now. No funny stuff during the night or Cheeseburger here will get ya!" Bait and Irving looked over at Cheeseburger. His hind leg was over his head and his nose up his butt.

"Oops," Cheeseburger said, quickly dropping his leg back to the ground.

Irving paused a moment and looked pensively out to the street. "Very good chaps, you've got yourselves a new flat mate." Putting down his pocketbook, he took a look at his new surroundings. Dismal, but they would do. He immediately began to clean up his area. Bait and Cheeseburger watched curiously as Irving took a lace hanky from his bag and began to dust off his new walls. Next, he took out two blue blankets. After removing some garbage, he delicately placed one blanket evenly on the ground, perfectly marrying the cotton edges with the red alley bricks. He took the other blanket and folded it evenly four times into a soft, cushy bed. It was fluffed exactly three times before he gently laid it down. Finally, Irving retrieved a yellow, silk blouse, which he glued to the walls with bubble gum forming a charming awning over his lovely abode. Beside him, he placed an old coffee tin down as his bedside table. Complete with a dimly lit candle and a sweet Fig Newton, Irving was finally ready for sleep.

"What da heck's going on here?" Bait cried. "Whadaya think this is? A four star Alley?"

"Why, no. I...," Irving stumbled.

"Yeah, maybe we should read you a bedtime story," Cheeseburger carried on, cackling like an idiot.

"Well, that would be just lovely if...," Irving said.

"Awe, come on. Just go to bed!" Bait added as he clutched his favorite brick. He slept with it almost every night. His little security brick.

Irving finished his evening snack and blew out his scented candle. "I'll see you bright and early in the morning," he said cheerfully, putting on his pointed, sleeping cap. "I couldn't be more thrilled to start over in a new city. This is all very exciting for me. You see, I..."

Life Four

"Shut up!" grunted Cheeseburger, cuddled in his newspapers. Irving turned up his nose and drifted off to sleep, dreaming of all the wondrous adventures he'd have in his new home.

On the other side of town, Romeo walked through the night air desperately searching for the old, abandoned schoolhouse. *It must be around here somewhere*, he said to himself. It's got to be. But the more Romeo wandered, the more lost he became. *Maybe I should have brought Fluffy*, he thought. *Awe, forget it. He wouldn't have come anyway.* Apparently, Romeo had given Fluffy the brush off one too many times. Fluffy stopped trying to be his friend. But now, Romeo began to tremble and wish he had Fluffy there with him. He was quickly realizing that being alone wasn't just boring, it was downright scary too.

So Romeo wandered on, down every dark and lonely street, past every eerie alleyway. Time ticked away fast. Suddenly, a loud screech caught his attention. A dirty, yellow cab slammed up against the curb. A wave of muddy water exploded all over the sidewalk dousing Romeo with a stinging chill. Romeo became so startled, his body flew into the gutter. "What the...?" he said, shaking the water from his ears.

The cab came to a sudden halt. Romeo sat up tall and tried to peek into the taxi's windows. They were tinted black and impossible to see through. Just then, the back door slowly creaked open. Romeo swallowed hard and long. His

Chapter Three

bottom lip quivered. He saw a slight trail of dust lingering from the inside. It smelled strange, like the inside of an old man's hat. As if in a trance, Romeo stepped forward, right for the open door. Suddenly he heard a voice. "Romeo," it said. "Romeo," he heard again. It was coming from inside the car. For a moment Romeo backed away. He looked up at a falling star and followed its reflection down a tiny stream of gutter water. As his eyes were led once again to the bewitched taxicab, Romeo called to the voice.

Hesitantly, Romeo took a step, then another, and another, finally reaching the edge of the car.

"Romeo," he heard once more. Romeo poked his head all the way inside. It was dark and stuffy. With intense trepidation, he slowly crept up onto the dry, vinyl seat.

The door began to close all by itself with a creak. Romeo's heart stopped as he dared to peer at the driver for the first time. Two dark, haunting eyes stared at him from the rear view mirror. Two hands stretched over the steering wheel. Human hands. Romeo could tell. Animals didn't wear thick, golden rings. Then suddenly, the voice. "Lost?" it asked.

"Uh...um," Romeo mumbled, troubled for words. Realizing he had made a terrible mistake, Romeo struggled hard to find a way out. Beads of sweat gathered on his head. But then, the driver turned around. His face leaned into the moonlight. It was human, all right. Old, worn, and wrinkled.

Life Four

Romeo was horrified.

"I'll take you to the old school, Romeo," the driver whispered. "It's around the corner."

Stunned, Romeo sunk into the crease of the seat, wedging himself between the vinyl cushions. Did he hear the man correctly? Was a person actually speaking to him? This was unprecedented. Romeo listened on.

"You are going to the school, right?" the voice asked, carefully driving down the street. "And to the second corner?"

"How...how do you know my n..name?" Romeo stuttered in disbelief, shocked that he was actually talking to a real, live person. After all, this was strictly forbidden. A Stick rule.

The elderly man looked straight ahead and stared down the long street. "I know a lot of things around here."

Romeo suctioned himself to the back of the seat. "This can't be happening! This can't be happening!" he cried, stuffing his paws in his ears. "Wake up, Romeo!" he said to himself. "Wake up!"

Suddenly the cab came to a final halt. Romeo lifted his head from his paws. The windows were foggy, the air crisp. "This is the place," the mystery driver said. "They're waiting for you."

"What? Who?" Romeo asked.

The yellow door slowly creaked open. A cool breeze shot through the cab knocking Romeo on his back. He saw the neon word *fare* near the driver, blinking bright red. "What's that?" Romeo

Chapter Three

asked, quickly pointing to the red letters.

"Forget about it. Just get out," the driver explained, his back still to Romeo. "You'll pay me someday."

Romeo didn't understand. "Huh?" he uttered. "What do you mean?"

But the driver didn't budge. His tired, sunken eyes glared back at Romeo from the rear view mirror. Romeo felt his cold stare and turned to the open door, quickly jumping outside. The car sped off down the street, its door waving in the wind.

Romeo stood alone in the hazy, evening fog. His ears barely poked through the top of the smoky layer. He coughed the mist out of his way. In the distance he heard a loud clock. Ding! Ding! Ding! It rang nine times to be exact.

Nine o'clock, Romeo said to himself. *I better get moving.*

From deep in the fog, Romeo couldn't see a thing. No cars. No buildings. Not even a single working street lamp. He didn't know which way to go. His heart started to pound. All around him creepy night noises echoed from down the long, empty streets. Nobody lived in this area, not anymore at least. It was the most deserted part of the city. Some say there were just too many 'accidents'. Particularly at the old school where he was heading. It was no surprise it had closed down two years earlier when nine children turned up missing. The principal skipped town in a hurry.

Life Four

Very suspicious.

Romeo stood shivering in the night air, when all of a sudden the fog seemed to mystically drift apart forming a hollow, grey tunnel. Romeo's eyes bugged out of his head. His heart leapt from his chest. A whisper of wind nudged him forward on a crazy pattern of swirls and whirls. His paws marched along the wet concrete up some strange sidewalk. Unable to see around the fog, he drifted on, moving by way of his unmistakable feline curiosity.

Suddenly, the fog closed in again. His path filled with more of the murky vapor. Romeo became blinded. Just as the mist reached its heaviest, gagging Romeo, it strangely began to clear and rolled away from him in waves. Romeo looked down and noticed he was paw deep in yucky, soggy mud. As the fog continued to dissipate, dark shadows and strange shapes filled the air like black spirits. Above, the moon hung in the clouds glowing misty green, and Romeo could finally see.

He was standing right in the center of the old school yard. It stood still like a tired, worn out ghost. He felt a chill crawl up his back as creepy noises echoed from the playground. A heavy silence drifted somewhere in between. Suddenly, he heard a haunting creak and immediately turned his head. Swaying gently in the air on their rusted, brown chains, were four old, lonely swings. Their torn, leather seats hinted of the once blue paint the

Chapter Three

children happily swung on. Beyond the swings was a dented, metal slide. A large corroded hole sat smack dab in the middle, devouring any unsuspecting kid who sailed down its trunk. More forgotten toys and equipment littered the abandoned grounds like a graveyard. A splintered, broken sea-saw, withered deflated balls, mangled jungle gym bars, and buried tricycles. Severed doll heads and twisted army men were among the casualties. A sudden pinch flared in Romeo's belly. He could almost feel the lost children, sense their eerie presence in this horrid place. It scared him and intrigued him at the same time. He had to continue.

Up ahead, Romeo was able to make out a large, dangling sign. SUBWAY, it buzzed in broken neon lights. Romeo knew that's where he needed to go. He would have to walk across the field of dead toys, a morgue of lost innocence. He took in a deep breath and began his journey.

Across the wilted leaves he crept, careful not to stir a thing. To his left was the dark shadow of the old, school building itself. The heavy, brick walls were lined with broken windows. Dozens of them. Though Romeo didn't look, he sensed young eyes peeking out at him through the jagged glass. He picked up his pace. Ahead, he could still faintly see the sleeping subway sign.

As he crossed the edge of the playground and approached the subway station, Romeo suddenly heard a child's laugh coming from behind. He whipped his head around. The laugh

Chapter Three

stopped. All Romeo could see was the wall of fog that had moved itself back into the schoolyard. Whoever belonged to that laugh was in there... somewhere.

Romeo rubbed his eyes and took long, deep breaths, clutching his chest with his paw. The large subway sign fell off its hinges with a loud crash right at Romeo's paws. He flinched back, his heart racing faster than before. He walked hesitantly down the few steps to the entrance. Like the school, the station was dark and deserted. Closed. A howling wind zipped past him and shot through the broken door frame. Romeo gulped hard and journeyed inside.

The station was so silent, Romeo could almost hear his own heartbeat. All around him were empty, torn seats and broken tiles. The ticket booth sat oddly abandoned, old pricing lists still taped to the window. The turnstiles had corroded shut, and a thick layer of greenish mold grew from the remnants of a once welcomed concession stand. The walls were covered in strands of cobwebs, and the ceiling had large, yellow stains. Romeo walked down the long, empty platform carefully avoiding the broken glass that lay scattered all over the floor. Now and then a roach scurried by, but not the kind of roach he wanted to eat. These were skinny and slimy and oozing in sludge. No wonder the rats wouldn't eat them either.

Romeo made his way down to the tracks. They hadn't been used in years. All the current

Life Four

trains had been rerouted from this spooky part of town. Romeo marveled at the ghostly sights, when all of a sudden something caught his attention. On the far side of the tracks, the small vent door suddenly swung open with a piercing creak. "Who's there?" Romeo shouted as he jumped. No one answered.

From where he stood, Romeo could only see into a black, dismal abyss. As he shivered on the platform staring at the open vent, he knew what he had to do. "That's the second corner," he whispered with a gulp. "Down there is the second corner." With hesitant steps, Romeo slowly walked to the open vent. In the distance, he heard the familiar whistle of an approaching subway train. But how could that be? He turned his head and saw bright headlights.

Chapter Four

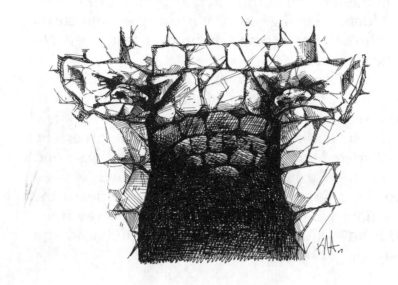

Fearing for his life, Romeo dashed inside the vent and out of harm's way. He clung to the metal bars from the other side and waited for the train to rumble by.

It was an old, black subway train, three cars long barrelling down the tracks like a panther. Thick, choking smoke billowed from its top. Massive dents pockmarked its sides. The train slammed to a screeching stop, pinching Romeo's eardrums like tweezers. It sat there silently in a windy cloud of dust, almost like it was waiting for something to happen. With a gnawing hesitation, Romeo stuck his head out of the vent door and looked at the train. The windows were black, and it appeared empty. Romeo's pulse doubled as his curiosity tripled. But before he could peek out any farther to see who was there, the doors shut. Slam! The train was off. Romeo pulled his head back as the locomotive flew out of sight, scattering old papers and cigarette butts in its path. Romeo was terrified. What mess had he gotten himself into this time? "Bubastis, if you're out there, please help me!" he murmured.

Once the train was out of view, Romeo turned back to see where this vent would lead him. He crept through the cave-like passage reaching a set of wooden, rickety stairs. At the very top, he held on tightly to the low, rusted rail that bolted into the mucky wall. Below, Romeo could see nothing but darkness. All that lay before him was a mystery. *I'm not going down there*, he thought. But a sudden chilling wind slapped him down the long staircase against his will and into the dismal unknown.

Romeo landed face down on the stairway, breaking a tooth. He screamed in agony as the broken molar shot out of his mouth. It soared down, down the long blackness until Romeo finally heard the tiniest ding of it hitting the cavern floor. His gums throbbing, he suctioned his body close to the rail and tiptoed the rest of the way down, hearing only the creak of the wooden stairs.

Suddenly, a hint of light glowed from behind an intricate series of stones. It blinked on and off,

Chapter Four

almost sending Romeo into a hypnotic trance. He followed the light to a large wall of heavy rocks. On either side of the wall were two ancient stone heads, bat heads. Their jade green eyes stared right through him. Filled with curiosity, Romeo felt one of the carved heads. Instantly, a stone door shifted on its gritty bottom. Romeo gasped watching it open all the way.

Through the door, Romeo felt a warm, dry heat wrap around his body. "Come here, my child," an elderly, female voice suddenly beckoned. "Come in."

"Who's that?" Romeo shivered. "Who's talking to me?"

Just then, the withered shape of a bat slowly came into focus. Romeo rubbed his eyes hard and saw the small, grey bat hanging upside down from a long, metal pipe. There was nothing else around save for some cobwebs and shriveled lemon rinds. Romeo hesitantly stepped closer, squinting his eyes and twitching his ears. He quivered suddenly realizing this bat had four wings! Each had long, sharp, golden symbols. Romeo stared, knowing for sure he was in Vent City, for this was no ordinary bat. It was a mutant. But weren't all the V.C. mutants gone? Romeo looked up. The bat's eyes glowed green and intimidating, its face withered and drawn.

"Who are you, and why are you here?" the bat abruptly asked.

Romeo flinched back. His heart racing

around his insides. "What?" he blurted. "Who are you? W..what's g..going on?" he stuttered.

All of a sudden, a small weasel stepped out of the darkness.

"Don't mind him, he won't bother you," the bat said. "Marlow goes everywhere with me."

"Marlow," Romeo whispered. "Marlow."

From the looks of him, Marlow was old, though not as old as the bat. He had a nappy, brown coat matted in a tangled mess of knots and burrs. Romeo noticed his strange limp, walking as if he had a wooden leg, a peg leg perhaps.

"Are you Trixie?" Romeo finally asked. He knew he had struck a chord by the bat's expression.

"Silence!" Trixie suddenly shouted. "I have had enough of you! I don't do favors for little pussy cats!"

Romeo flinched back several paws. "But... but...I haven't asked for anything yet!"

"I said silence! Get out of my cavern!" she wailed. "Out! Out!"

"But..."

"Out!"

"I need to do a job for Hog! I have to bring food to his colony!" Romeo exploded.

Instantly, Trixie swung back and forth and shut her green eyes, mumbling some sort of gibberish to herself. The whole thing was very weird.

"Yes, I know about Hog," Trixie finally began. "But I don't do favors for free. You must prove your worthiness and determination first."

"Huh?" Romeo gasped. "What's that mean?"

"Silence!"

Romeo sat still.

"You are Romeo, aren't you?" Trixie inquired to Romeo's surprise.

"Yes," Romeo replied.

"Ah-hah!" she nodded, staring up into space. "Then I will help you once you have done something for me first," Trixie said calmly with her four wings wrapped tightly around her body.

"What?" Romeo asked. "What could I possibly do for you?"

"Bring me the collar of a dog," she began. "I don't like dogs! They killed my sisters! I want the collar of a dog, a dead dog."

Romeo stood back in horror. "How am I supposed to....What?" he exploded. "Where am I going to get a dead dog's collar? I don't even have a collar! It would be easier getting the food!"

Trixie eyed him sternly. "Bring me the collar if you expect any help from me! Now go!" With his long, lanky paw, Marlow pointed to the exit. Romeo turned away then snapped back with a sudden thought. When he did, Trixie and Marlow were gone. No one was there.

Romeo bolted past the stone bats and back toward the vent. In a flash, he flew through but instead of falling right onto the station floor, he shot forward over the edge of a thick, smoky wall. "Ahhh!" screamed Romeo, plummeting downward, wind zipping through his fur. Falling deeper into the darkness, he heard the same piercing child's laughter he had heard earlier. With a thump, he landed on the wet, marshy ground of the old, broken down schoolyard. Romeo dashed as fast as he could for the street until the station was clear out of sight.

Romeo raced down the deserted avenues. It was cold and very dark outside. Up ahead he saw a warm light coming from an all night TV repair shop. In the window blazed an old black and white. The local evening news was on. Romeo leaned against the window as he watched the broadcast out of pure curiosity. He listened closely. "City dwellers beware!" the reporter warned. "Buggles Flannigan is on the loose! The notorious catnapping bank robber has escaped! I repeat! Buggles Flannigan has escaped!"

Romeo squinted at the photo of the man in question on the TV screen. *That's Calvin's old napper,* he remembered. *He's supposed to be in jail!* Romeo wondered if his old friend Calvin had once again fallen into the hands of doom.

"Mr. Flannigan was due in court this week on three counts of catnapping, two charges of bank robbery, and a theft charge for stealing an old lady's baguette," the reporter said very quickly. "Mr. Flannigan is facing a lengthy prison sentence if found guilty. He was last seen in the pickle line of the city jail where he was being held without bail. He is believed to be armed and dangerous.

If anyone has any information, please contact authorities at...blah, blah, blah."

As if there isn't enough to worry about around here, Romeo said to himself with a long, heavy sigh.

"And hear this, my faithful listeners," the reporter added, "Buggles left this chilling message written on his cell wall. Flannigan rules!"

Romeo leaned up against the cold bricks, took a careful look around, and zoomed back into the night.

Bait awoke from a terrible nightmare around midnight layered in a cold, cold sweat. In his warped mind he dreamed he was leaping headfirst into a tiny tub of Smugglers Salty Cat Food. Shaken and very thirsty, he slapped Cheeseburger awake with a pressing idea. "We're goin' to the Glitterbox!" he shouted in Cheeseburger's puffy ear. "Come on, fatty! Let's go! I'm thirsty!"

Cheeseburger rolled over onto his side. His nostrils flared as he snored in ultimate slumber.

"Wake up!" Bait cried.

Cheeseburger's eyes cracked open. He smacked the gooey cake on his lips together. "Wha...?" he mumbled. "Bait? Go back to bed." With his paw, Cheeseburger pulled up an old, soggy newspaper and cuddled his body against it. Bait snatched it away and bonked Cheeseburger on the head.

"To the Glitteroom!" Bait squealed again, finishing with an explosive sneeze.

Life Four

"Are you crazy?" Cheeseburger asked, rubbing newspaper ink off his orange head. "It's sleepy time! Besides, have you forgotten what happened last year?"

"Big deal! Old news!" Bait whined. "I'm thirsty!"

At the stylish, elegantly decorated corner of the alley, Irving awoke from the annoying bantering. Amongst a sprinkling of pine needles, he stuffed two Greek olives in his ears and attempted to fall back to sleep.

Bait finally got his way, something Fidel never would have believed. Soon the three males were off to the local Alley watering hole. Cheeseburger and Irving reluctantly followed closely behind. Cheeseburger clutched a scrap of the newspaper he so loved, Irving with an olive in his left ear.

The three Alleys arrived and entered through the old, rusted pipe still sloppily wrapped in soup can labels. The joint was just starting to rock, as it usually did after midnight. The drinkers drank, the nip addicts nipped, and the party roared on. The full-time gals were already sauntering devilishly around on the greasy stage by the time Bait and his cohorts arrived.

"This place is dreadful," Irving grimaced from behind the wall of purple, shimmery tinsel, a piece of it whistling in and out of his nose.

"Let's get dis party goin'!" Bait howled, pushing Irving clear out of his way. As he boogied toward the bar, a large furball smacked him on the top of his head, knocking him to the ground.

"Getta load a da' tough guy!" Big grumbled, one of the more fierce up-and-coming Alleys. He cleared his throat for another furball. "He tinks he's a tough guy!"

Big, he got the name because of his hefty size, laughed a deep and hollow laugh, others following his lead. Bait sizzled at the door, trying hard to maintain an air of coolness even though he desperately wanted to attack the shimmery tinsel. He made sure to appear unfazed by the huge, gooey wad stuck to the top of his head like a silly hat. Casually leaning against the far wall, a snide, sneaky grin cracked across his face. Cheeseburger leaned against the wall too but slid down the slimy bricks knocking himself and Bait onto the beer-splattered floor. Big and the others erupted into hysterics.

"Dat's a good one, Bait," Big hurled, clenching his belly. Suddenly, he noticed Irving. "Hey, fellas!" he cried pointing his paw in merriment. "Check out the new guy, Mr. Fancy Pants!"

Everyone's eyes went to Irving. Sure enough, ignoring Bait's warnings, he was wearing his very striking silk, paisley cat pants especially made for him. Irving held his chin high in the air as everyone chided him. "Fancy Pants! Fancy Pants!" The inebriated Alleys focused harder on his blurry trousers and roared with more laughter than before. Even Bait was laughing.

Life Four

"I'm hardly amused," Irving wallowed, turning his chin to the air.

From the sticky ground, Bait knocked Cheeseburger out of his way as he yelled to Big and the boys. "We're just as tough as any of yous!" he said. Cheeseburger moved to get up and unexpectedly expelled a large cloud of meaty gas from his rump. He blushed under his flaring nostrils and grinned.

"Uh, sorry," he mumbled.

Big and his buddies stuck out their bottoms and began mimicking Cheeseburger's unpleasant doings while Irving and Bait plugged their noses at the noxious stink.

Big swaggered up to the uninvited and stood directly over their heads. "Without Fidel around, you's not much good, is ya?" Big snapped. He was right. Without Fidel, Bait lost whatever milli-ounce of respect he once had.

Finally mustering up some courage, for he wasn't a complete waste, Bait stood tall. He bravely opened his mouth to speak when Cheeseburger's tail smacked him in the jaw. "Watch it!" Bait screamed.

"Sorry," Cheeseburger whined.

"I thought you're not allowed here anymore," Big reminded. "Dat's what Max says! Remember?" Apparently, about a year prior Bait had a few too many drinks one night and hassled some of the dancers. Of course, everybody hassled the dancers, but Bait had been the only one to do

Chapter Four

something just plain stupid. Laughing like a mad man, he ran into their dressing room and threw all their costumes onto the floor. Just as he started putting on a fancy headpiece, he barfed right on the pile of red boas. They were ruined, the night's performance cancelled. Cheeseburger listened horrified from the bar at the wretching sound coming from the dressing room. He and Bait were pelted with furballs hard as bullets, thrown out on their bottoms and told never to return to the Glitterbox again. Until this night, they hadn't dared.

"Awe, come on, Big," Bait whined. "Dat was a long time ago. Besides, I'll make it worth your while."

Big surveyed the club. Some of the females were hiding their digs. "Oh, yeah?" Big asked. "How so?"

"How's about a chug-a-lug contest?" Bait suggested.

Cheeseburger nudged Bait in the side with his fat shoulder. "Maybe we should just get outta here," he whispered. "I feel kinda sick anyway." Irving adjusted the elastic on his pants and watched with heavy anticipation.

"I betcha we can out drink any three of yous," Bait bragged. Fact of the matter was, Bait had been boozing it up pretty good over at Smelly's Bar and had a good shot at winning. He'd be a king, to himself at least. "If we win, we stays. If we lose, we goes."

Life Four

"You're on!" Big said confidently as he pulled Max, the owner, into the ring.

"Rack 'em up, Sally," Max ordered his finest waitress. "Three rounds for everybody!"

Irving's eyes widened.

Cheeseburger watched closely as Sally poured the beer. It was thicker and warmer than usual. "Duh, I can't do it," Cheeseburger said to Bait. "I tink we should split. Let's just go to Smelly's. Thumb's got some new tunes."

Big pushed aside his plate of string and weeds and grabbed a tight hold of his first mug. Bait snatched his brew and leaned in closely to Big's bulging eyes. Cheeseburger and Irving shivered behind him.

"Irving, Cheeseburger, grab a mug," Bait roared, his drink rattling in his paws.

Irving looked at the murky, putrid liquid. "I say, old fellow," he began, "I do enjoy a sip of goat milk now and again, but I'm not much of a fan of this sort of refreshment."

"Awe, shut up and drink!" Bait ordered.

"One, two, three!" Sally counted, holding her scarf above her head. "Let the games begin!"

Bait and Cheeseburger were off to a good start. But not Irving. He was staring blankly into the mug, watching his blurry reflection bounce around. Big, Max, and Mustard were drowning in their second beer. Bait reached for his third.

"We're winning! We're winning!" Cheeseburger hollered, jumping up and down and knocking over the beers.

Sally ran for more. Irving continued to stare.

Suddenly, Big and his team began to catch up. They were gulping down the swill like there was no tomorrow. "Keep pounding!" Big shouted.

Cheeseburger tried his hardest, but the furballs were welling up inside him. Pretty soon, his whole body began to shake, and a deep, grumbling gurgle began to rumble from his stomach. His lips turned blue, and his eyes bugged out. Everyone froze and watched as his body puffed up like a blowfish.

"Look out!" Mustard shouted. "He's gonna burst!"

Like a tidal wave, all the malted liquid Cheeseburger had in him exploded from every orifice in his body, dousing everyone in sight. Bait was mortified.

"We've got 'em!" Big hollered with splattered beer dripping from his ears. He looked Bait deeply in the eyes and wailed, "I told you, Bait! You're nothing without Fidel!"

Bait boiled with anger. "That does it!" he cried. Pushing Cheeseburger and his pukey breath aside, Bait grabbed hold of Irving's neck and shoved his nose into the mug. "Drink!" he screamed.

"I...I...I...," Irving studdered.

"Just do it!" Bait insisted. "I can't let 'em talk to me like dat!"

Irving reluctantly began pounding the

drinks. They went down like sewer water, yucky and gross. "Who could drink this wretched slop?" he slurred with a gag.

"Keep going!" Bait roared, watching Max and the others closely.

Filled with new adrenalin, Bait and Irving sucked down their mugs as Cheeseburger gagged and gurgled on the floor.

But Irving was slowing down. His tongue stuck out longer and longer, and his posture sunk lower and lower. "No more!" he belched loudly.

"Do it!" Bait stammered.

"But..."

"Drink it, Fancy Pants!" Bait snapped.

Irving obeyed. He was afraid not to. After a few more forced gulps, his nose began to turn a pale shade of green. His beer fell from his paw and crashed to the ground. He stumbled and wobbled around, knocking right into a table ripping his fine silk pants on a rusted nail. Everyone watched.

"Don't stop now!" Bait hollered at Irving, believing they somehow still had a chance.

With every ounce of strength he had, Irving grabbed a beer from Sally's tray and shoved it in his trembling face. As soon as the first tiny drop fell on his tongue, he collapsed to the ground. Bait raced over.

"Get up!" he roared. "Don't let them win! The dancers! Think of the dancers!"

But it was no use. Irving didn't care about the dancers. In fact, he didn't care about anything.

Chapter Four

He lay dead on the floor from a beer overdose like a scaled fish, soggy and lifeless. His little body just couldn't take it as his second life slipped away on the hard, hard floor.

"Whadya do to him?" Cheeseburger squealed.

Bait stood frozen. He looked around in all directions. Nobody moved. The silence was penetrating. "Look what ya did, Bait!" Big hollered. "Ya killed Mr. Fancy Pants!"

Everyone exploded into laughter.

"Wake up, ya ol' grouch!" Bait squealed shaking Irving up and down.

"Is he dead?" Cheeseburger mumbled, beer dripping from his nose.

Yes, Irving was dead, and for the second time in one night, all because of Bait and his stupid need to prove his manly prowess.

After the hilarity died down, the music erupted, the females resumed performing, and the party continued. "Get out and stay out this time!" Max roared in Bait's direction. "I don't wanna see you in here ever again!" Bait and Cheeseburger shamefully dragged Irving's body across the floor and quietly slipped out into the night.

Back in their alley, Cheeseburger tossed Irving's lifeless body into his corner and got himself ready for bed.

Bait flattened his fur with a slick layer of spit and sat down on a pile of garbage, clutching his favorite brick. Suddenly, a noise caught him off guard. He sat up straight and listened.

"Where ya going?" Cheeseburger asked from under his newspapers.

"Be right back," Bait answered. He walked through the alley to the street and slowly turned the corner out of sight. Cheeseburger waited.

After about two long minutes, Bait emerged from the haze. His body shook and jittered, and his eyes were fixed open. A few hairs stood straight up on his funny, bumpy head like weeds.

"What's da matter, Bait?" Cheeseburger asked. "You seen a ghost or somethin'?"

Bait slowly turned to face him. "Rats," he said. "Ugly rats!"

"Rats? Yum! Where?"

Bait slithered back to bed and lay still. The sight of that rat would haunt him all night long.

Chapter Five

It was one in the morning, and Romeo was lost...again. He looked up into the night sky. The moon was hanging like a diamond, pretty and bright.

Romeo zigzagged through the empty streets looking for the Factory. He glared at the unfamiliar buildings and sneered into the darkened alleyways. As much time as he had invested on the city streets, there was still so much he had never seen, so much yet to explore. The city was big, bigger than Romeo, and bigger than his inflated ego. Its edges were boundless, without certainty. As fearful as that could be, it brought an element of mystery and excitement into the never ending dramas of the city. Something Romeo and every other city animal was very accustomed to. Queen Elizabeth always warned him about going into foreign areas. "Stay where you know," she would say. It was too late for that now.

The more Romeo walked, the more lost he became, drifting farther and farther away from the Factory. Not that he had such an aching desire to go back there, but being homeless and alone was not an option. Not for a Stick, and certainly not in this part of town. He was tired and scared. If he didn't sleep, he'd never get that food for those darn rats. Wandering around in the dark tugged at his rusted heartstrings and made him long for his old friends and, of course, Dennis. He had never stopped missing Dennis. So he cried. Crying was something he hadn't done much lately. That's what happens when you shut down.

Awe, hell, Romeo said to himself. *I gotta get some sleep. I can't take it anymore!* He stood in the dead center of a quiet intersection. All alone. The street lights above him blinked red and green, while the yellow blazed strong. In a pinch, he could always hide somewhere safe, like under something. He had Mr. Shadow's City Survival class to thank for that at least.

From the middle of the road Romeo spotted a blue mailbox. It would do, at least for the next few hours. He leaped around a large puddle of car grease and darted over to check it out. Hearing a strange sound, he bolted under it. Was it Buggles?

Chapter Five

Hog? A monster? Romeo poked his nose out from underneath the rusted box and saw the backside of a small, old gent bouncing down the street on a rickety, green bicycle. No Hog. No monster. Just a codger out for a late night ride.

Romeo breathed a sigh of relief and huddled into a tight ball. He was safe for now. As he lay there thinking about his troubles, he was suddenly blinded by two shining headlights. There hadn't been a car on the road for hours, not in this deserted part of town.

Romeo inched out from under the mailbox to get a closer look. It was that taxi again! As it came to a dead halt, Romeo felt the same bubbling sense of alarm.

The taxi door creaked open. It idled there humming on its four black tires, waiting for him. With odd curiosity, Romeo slinked out from his nook and crawled into the cab. He saw the same man as before. His dark eyes never blinking, only staring straight ahead. Always straight ahead. His bony hands stretched over the steering wheel wrapped in thick, chunky, gold rings. The black crud under his fingernails had been there for days, maybe weeks. Romeo wiggled his bottom into position on the red, torn seat. He reached over and closed the door. In an instant, the driver and the taxi sped off.

From the back seat, Romeo watched the city race by in a blur of colorful, swirling lights. Where was the cab taking him? He pressed his nose to the

Life Four

cold window and licked the glass. It tasted funny, like dirt. He found a small, metal compartment near the door handle and stuck his paw in. It was an ashtray full of rotted, old cigarettes. When he pulled his paw away, it was covered in gray ash, like some of the higher floors of the Factory.

The haunting ride seemed to go on for hours. Romeo found it hard to concentrate on anything, but after a while he began to recognize some familiar sights. If he was right, the Factory would be to his left, two blocks. He looked out the window as he felt the cab turn.

The taxi came to a stop at the front entrance of the Factory. Romeo grimaced out the window for a moment at the building he so loved and hated at the same time. It was now too filled with bitter memories. Romeo wanted nothing to do with it, still it was all he had.

The taxi door opened as mysteriously as it had before. Romeo wiggled his body over to the far edge and hopped out without looking back at the driver. As the cab sped off, a slap of wind knocked Romeo to the ground. From the concrete, he watched as the car sailed down the long, lonely street out of sight.

Inside, some die hard Sticks were busily preparing for tomorrow's opening ceremony. *Losers*, Romeo thought.

Tabitha spotted him behind a wall of hanging blue streamers. He looked tired and confused. "Hey, Romeo!" she called, still clinging to the hope he'd lighten up. "Where've you been?"

"What's it to you?" Romeo stopped in the middle of the room. "I don't wanna be a part of this silly party anyway!"

The other Sticks in the room heard and knew things weren't getting any better. Their beloved Romeo seemed gone forever.

Romeo made his way to the tiny, blue door leading to Waldo's photography lab. Though it hadn't been functioning as a lab for quite some time, Waldo kept it as his office, just in case. Actually, Romeo slept in it at night. He and his father were usually the only ones who slept at the Factory because they didn't belong to any people. Occasionally Candle slept on a pillow when it rained, but she wasn't really a Stick. At first, Romeo would stay up with her and talk late into the night, but lately he hardly paid her any attention.

Early the next morning, Romeo cracked open his crusty eyes. It had been a long night, and he didn't get much rest. He stretched out his two front paws and yawned wide enough to suck in a hundred flies. His father would be up soon, and would surely be looking for him. If he didn't get moving, Romeo knew he would get stuck in one of those father-son talks, and he was in no mood for that.

Romeo rubbed his eyes clean and noticed a small blur in front of him creeping around on the floor. He shook his head awake to see Octavian, the spider. Though all Factory spiders looked the same, this one seemed different. After all, Octavian was practically the Factory mascot. Romeo's tummy grumbled at the anticipation of his spider breakfast, but something stopped him. Something that made Romeo just watch. He didn't swat at Octavian, didn't tease and taunt him into a game of kitty soccer, he just stared.

Like a daredevil mountain climber, Octavian crawled right up Romeo's leg up to the tip of his wet nose. Any other spider would have been long gone by now, ground and pulverized down the gullet of Romeo's body, but Octavian was being spared. Why?

As Romeo stared hypnotically at Octavian's bean size body, Octavian lifted one of his hairy legs, stepped down and began to walk toward the blue lab door. Curiously, Romeo followed. Octavian crept under it and disappeared.

Romeo creaked open the door and ran his eyes along the dark, wooden floor over to the couch, his favorite couch. All around him were boxes of streamers, celebration signs, and colorful party hats. Candle was still asleep, probably dreaming of the big day ahead. Romeo continued to look around when he heard a noise. "Dad?" he whispered. Romeo swung his head toward the new elevator, currently going through a battery of safety tests, praying not to see his father marching into the room. Luckily for him, it had only been the rustle of the wind outside.

Life Four

Again, Romeo spotted Octavian now standing in front of the basement door. The basement was a forbidden place, though nobody knew why. Even Mr. Sox never went down there. During the Vent City revolt, a slew of Alleys were forced down and viscously maimed by the dogs, and no one dared mentioned the basement after that. The door always remained shut. Romeo reasoned that whatever was down in that pit of darkness couldn't have been any worse than anything he'd already seen. After all, he had been to Vent City and two corners. As far as Sticks go, he had seen it all.

Octavian bounced on the tips of his legs and slipped under the wooden basement door. He was a spider. He could do that sort of thing. Romeo was too big for that stunt. If he wanted to investigate, he'd have to open the door. He stuck his paws under and pulled with all his might, but it wouldn't budge. He yanked and tugged, and finally the door creaked open with a loud jolt. Just as Romeo stuck his nose inside, he heard Candle. She was awake.

Candle rolled over on her side and faced him. "Romeo?" she whispered with her eyes half open and glossy. "Wh...what are you doing?"

"Shhhh!" Romeo snapped. "You'll wake my dad. Go back to sleep."

Candle's head fell back to the couch. "But where are you....," she began to say as she drifted off in mid-question.

Chapter Five

Romeo waited a few seconds to make sure she was asleep. Hearing her little snore, he returned to the basement and hesitantly stepped inside the dark entryway. The heavy door slammed behind him with a loud boom. Romeo shuddered from the noise, tumbling down a long flight of stairs hoping the door hadn't woken everyone up. Bonk! Bonk! Bonk! Surely he had crushed that spider. Awe, drat! Romeo cursed only to find it wasn't so as the sudden shadow of a massive spider came prowling around the corner. It seemed to grow bigger and bigger as it got closer and closer. Soon, it nearly filled up the entire room! Romeo crouched into a ball and felt a chill run up his spine building a paranoia of terror in him that was unstoppable. But then, a sudden tickle on his paw slowed his throbbing heart and faced Romeo head on. There was no giant spider, no monster ready to devour Romeo into itty-bitty pieces. It was only Octavian and his magnified shadow. "You again," Romeo sighed. Octavian allowed Romeo to lift him all the way to his face. He looked delicious. Those juicy legs, meaty middle filled with succulent innards. Romeo would have preferred taunting him and chasing him around for a while, but he was far too hungry. He had decided to chuck Octavian and all his yumminess right into his drooling mouth, when he suddenly saw something strangely suspicious. On the far side of the room where the sunlight was poking through, a garden of cardboard boxes lay sloppily on the floor. *A bunch of old boxes? That's*

Life Four

the big mystery about this place? Romeo remarked to himself. *Who cares about a bunch of boxes?* Forgetting about his arachnid breakfast, he put Octavian down to satisfy his curiosity instead.

Romeo inched closer. There were papers spilling from the boxes. His eyes panned across what looked like receipts and work orders from the by-gone days when the Factory made umbrellas. He stopped on something most unusual. A small white paper with a child's drawing on it. But there were no children working at the umbrella factory. Romeo snagged the paper and brought it closer to him. It was of a family. There was a house, a boy and a girl, mom and dad, and under a big, green tree, a pretty, white cat. Romeo was about to walk away when he noticed some scribbling in the corner. It said, Queen Elizabeth, written in little blue letters. Perhaps she had drawn this picture when she was a young kitten, and somehow it ended up in the basement. Naw, it's just a stupid drawing, he told himself. Forget about it. Romeo stepped on the paper and walked deeper into the basement toward a room near the back.

He trudged through the mountain of more papers and headed straight for its open door revealing a small, damp recess. Romeo looked cautiously around and came across a very gruesome sight. A pile of bones! Gross! he said to himself mustering up some courage to slowly creep closer. Sure enough, in the dark and far corner lay dozens of rotten, maggot-filled bones! All sizes! Even teeth. Could these be Alley bones? he questioned remembering the Alleys who disappeared into the basement during the Vent City revolt. But there were other skeletons too. Some obviously birds, other larger ones surely dogs.

Romeo gagged, trying not to inhale the wicked smell. But being the cat he was, he tossed around a few maggots like soccer balls. They jumped and wiggled and started a whole wave of action. "Whoa!" Romeo shrieked out loud. As the maggots scrambled around, he spotted something shiny and gold.

Romeo moved forward to steal it, when a sudden buzzing noise startled him, catapulting him nearly five feet in the air, then crashing down. Flop! Bones shooting in all directions. "Gross!" Romeo cried, maggots scurrying through his fur. "Get offa me! Get away!" He flailed his paws around like a mad beast, but the more Romeo moved, the deeper he sank into the pit of remains. The bones were swallowing him up like quicksand.

Then Romeo heard that buzzing noise again. He peeked over a femur and saw... "A fly!" he howled. "That's all? A stupid fly?" Romeo could certainly handle that. Minus his recent paranoia, he climbed his way out and peered over the bones. He immediately dug through the maggots for that golden object until he found it. This is a collar, he thought, holding it tightly in his paw.

Life Four

Chapter Five

A dog's collar! No cat could wear this, not even Uncle Fred! Romeo was right. He was holding a dog's collar. But who's? In fact, as Romeo went on with his search, he noticed two other collars. Then three! Then four! This is great! I'll take one of these to Trixie!

At that moment, Romeo heard footsteps coming from above followed by a familiar voice. "Romeo? Romeo, is that you?" his father called from the basement door. "Romeo? You better not be down there!"

Romeo froze. His father would lecture him for sure. Nobody was ever allowed in the basement. Candle! That blasted Candle! Romeo thought. She must have told my father. He quickly hid in the first garbage can he saw and waited, breathing hard. Octavian crawled up a wooden beam and watched.

Romeo could feel the vibrations of his father's pawsteps as he crawled down the stairs. "I know you're down here!" he blared with the sounds of disappointment. "Come out immediately!"

But Romeo stayed in the garbage can. He couldn't face his father. Not like this. In spite of his past string of troubles, hiding in the forbidden basement would surely ground him for life, or at least two lives.

Romeo heard the footsteps growing closer. His heart pounded faster. But as quickly as they had begun, the footsteps suddenly stopped.

Life Four

Carefully, Romeo stood on his hind legs and with his paws on the top rim of the can, he peeked over the edge with his nose. To his horror, his father's bulging eyes were staring back at him.

"Get out of there, Romeo!" Mr. Gamble insisted. "What do you think you're doing? This is not a playground!"

Romeo wrestled around in a panic soon knocking over the entire can. It sounded like bad drum practice. "What's the big deal, dad?" he echoed in his snotty teenage voice from inside the can as it rolled across the room.

Mr. Gamble stood as tall as he could. "What's the big deal?" he began as his face grew hotter and hotter. "You're not allowed down here! Just look around! This place is an accident waiting to happen!"

Romeo rolled his eyes. "No, it's not. Why can't I..."

"Because! That's why!" Mr. Gamble scolded. "I swear, Romeo! I don't know what's gotten into you lately! You're out of control!" Mr. Gamble huffed up the stairs. At the top, he turned and waited for Romeo.

Romeo knew he was wrong to rummage through the basement, but he couldn't understand why. What was the big deal about a bunch of old bones anyway?

"Did you think you were going to get away with this?" roared Mr. Gamble. "Did you think I wouldn't find out?"

Chapter Five

Romeo sauntered up the stairs with his nose snobbishly pointed in the air. He walked right past his father and back into the rec room. He'd have to come back for the collar. Mr. Gamble closed the basement door and shook his head in frustration.

That same morning Mr. Sox left his apartment with curled whiskers and hope. Dr. Think was expecting him for his first appointment. He didn't want to be late. It wasn't every day he had an appointment with Dr. Think. He was top of the line, cream of the crop, the best shrink in town. Dr. Think had been counselling Sticks for years. He helped them through their lives, their deaths, traumatic tragedies such as de-clawing, getting fixed, and separation anxiety. His office was in the big medical high rise on the north side of town near City Park. Mr. Sox had met him years earlier at a fishtail party and held a great deal of respect for him professionally. Mr. Sox knew Dr. Think was the only one who could help him to understand what was going on in Romeo's head.

Mr. Sox marched down the four blocks finally reaching 36 Medical Plaza. When no one was looking, he slid through the mail slot and dashed over to the far left wall. There, he could hoist himself into the mail chute and sail down to his appointment. The medical building had a very elaborate pharmacy in the basement. At any given moment, any doctor in the building could messenger down a prescription of choice. Within

Life Four

moments, the bottle would be delivered right up to the doctor's office. It was a primitive system, yes, but it worked well. Especially for Dr. Think and his thriving business.

It was 7:30 exactly. Mr. Sox carefully lifted the little door and crawled inside onto the small, steel platform. He was lucky. In another thirty minutes the place would be crawling with people. With his paws, Mr. Sox reached as far to the right as he could and pulled the two ropes one at a time. It was just like using the soup pot back at the Factory. He huffed all the way down to the garage level as his elderly arms ached while pulling those ropes. In fact, it seemed everything was getting a little harder with each day. At any rate Mr. Sox made it down smoothly and safely.

He stood in the gray, cement garage. It was drab and ugly. Every wall looked the same. Most offices weren't open yet, so there were only a few parked cars. Mr. Sox stood in the center and reached for his instructions, which he had written on a small piece of paper hidden under his collar. Find orange cone under fire hose. He looked hard. The garage was pretty dark and littered with all sorts of automotive junk, but soon he spotted a large, pointy orange cone, and sure enough, a fire hose. Within seconds Mr. Sox was entering Dr. Think's office located through a tiny slot in the janitor's closet just to the left of the cone.

Once inside Mr. Sox faced another problem. He didn't know which way to turn, and his directions ended with the cone. He scoured up and down at the dusty pipes and their dripping strings of debris. If he wasn't so afraid of being late, he would have loved to explore the territory. It was intriguing, even for an old geezer like himself. Suddenly, he heard a small voice over the pipes. He followed it to the left and around a sharp corner. On the pipe in front of him a large, metal license plate hung from two twisted pieces of wire. It read, Dr. Think, FMD. Feline Medical Doctor. Psychiatric Unit. This must be the place, he smiled, ducking under the swinging sign and through a small doorway.

"May I help you?" asked a flighty looking female from behind her desk made out of an old Crowman's Department Store shoebox. "Here to see the doctor?" she continued, filing her claws and licking her nose.

Before he answered, Mr. Sox took a quick glance around the office. There was a large pillow leaning up against the wall. Above it hung a picture of Smuggler's Salty Cat Food. The cat model in the ad was one of the doctor's most prestigious patients. Lots of problems, though. Apparently, Klaus, the model, was dealing with an identity crisis. He often believed he was Santa Claus. In fact, Dr. Think handled a lot of celebrities, even the famous Theodore from the old Gritty Kitty Pee Remover Company. Of course, Theodore skipped town after being beaten up by a bunch of Alleys.

In front of the pillow was an old crayon

box serving as a coffee table, although no Stick in his right mind liked coffee. On the table was a small thimble of yarn, one puffy ball, and two marbles. There used to be three, but somebody swallowed one. Next to the toys were a series of informative pamphlets. The Nip and You, SANK: Sticks Against Nipped Cats, and NIP, The Untold Truth.

"Yes, I'm here to see Dr. Think," Mr. Sox finally began. "I have a 7:30. My name is Sox."

Miss Angel, the receptionist, skimmed her schedule. "Ah, yes, right this way please."

Miss Angel led Mr. Sox through a small entryway and into Dr. Think's main office which was nestled between a couple of water pipes. Whenever someone upstairs flushed a toilet, a tidal wave rushed through the pipes making an awful racket. It wasn't ideal, but Dr. Think liked it a lot better than his last office at the meat factory. That place just smelled bad all the time.

Dr. Think wasn't in yet, so Mr. Sox was encouraged to lay on the couch and wait. "He'll be here soon," Miss Angel said.

Mr. Sox flopped onto the lumpy couch and looked around. It was an interesting place. He almost fell asleep when a voice came from behind. "Well, if it isn't the famous Mr. Sox." It was Dr. Think. He wore a simple bow tie and walked with a limp. "Right on time."

"Of course, I'm never late," Mr. Sox replied. "I'm a male of my word."

Chapter Five

"Good, good." Dr. Think sat down in his large beanbag chair and sifted through some papers. "Now let's get started. Time is food."

"Yes," Mr. Sox said gazing at the diploma on the wall. Bestowed Upon Dr. Thaddeus Think, FMD, City Medical College, read the napkin diploma. Dr. Think studied at the prestigious medical school's feline division on a full scholarship. It was a people college, of course, but the city animals knew how to get in and listen without being noticed. Sometimes they got caught because of their scent. A cat's smell is difficult to hide. Because of this, only four cats were allowed to attend each year, accepted by a very select panel. Many animals, not just the cats, attended the medical school. Birds, even dogs. Dr. Think was a star student often invited to lecture and share some yummy snacks.

"What seems to be the problem?" Dr. Think asked in a serious, doctoral tone.

Mr. Sox took in a slow, deep breath. "Well, it's not me. It's Romeo," Mr. Sox began, seated between two large lumps in the pillow. "It all started when..."

Dr. Think listened to the whole story. How Romeo came to the Factory, the brutal murder of his mother and brothers, his trouble with Fidel, the island, his relationship with Queen Elizabeth, and all the ugly rest. "...so you see, Dr. Think, I just don't know what to do with him. Nobody does. He's turned into a bitter disillusioned teenager."

Life Four

"Has he had any strange dreams?" Dr. Think asked curiously.

"Not that I am aware of."

"What's his relationship like with his father? Do you often see him sitting alone? Has he ever been known to try nip? Has he withdrawn socially? Does he talk to himself? When was the last time he groomed himself?"

As Mr. Sox opened his mouth to speak, the pipes went crazy, water gushing through like rapids. Toilets flushing left and right.

Dr. Think waited silently in his chair, twiddling the strings of his tie. "Sorry about that. There's always heavy activity early in the morning after the first cup of coffee," he explained. "Well, I have only this to say," he diagnosed in his deep, hearty voice. "The male's obviously given up on himself. There's nothing you can do."

"You've got to be kidding?" Mr. Sox cried. "You're a famous doctor! Haven't you got anything else to say?" Mr. Sox stood up and paced around the room. "He may have given up, but look at what he's been through. Surely there must be something we can do!"

"Listen, Sox, my professional opinion would be to just wait for him to snap out of it. He's young. He's going through that angry teenage stage. He won't listen to you anyway. He needs to figure things out for himself."

Mr. Sox shook his head with disappointment from behind his tiny bifocals. He had so hoped

77

Chapter Five

for some magical words that would turn Romeo around. Bring him back to life. Light that old fire in him once again. But Dr. Think was probably right. The truth was hard to hear. There was not much anybody could do. Teenagers! For the first time Mr. Sox, the wisest of all Sticks, felt helpless.

Sox left the small office dragging his tail on the ground. "That'll be two tuna cans," Miss Angel piped in from behind her desk.

"Send me a bill," Sox answered walking out the door, his shoulders hanging low.

Chapter Six

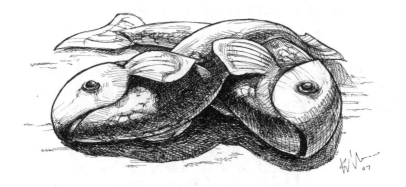

Octavian hoped Romeo wouldn't be in too much trouble for sneaking downstairs. Most spiders didn't care much about the cats for obvious reasons, but the Sticks had provided years of quality entertainment for Octavian. Actually, even though everyone called him Octavian, he was really Octavian IV. Fourth in line of a succession of great spiders. Octavian IV's great-great-great grandfather was the leader of the spider movement only a few years earlier, which had come at a time when spider morale was at an all time low. Things hadn't gone their way in years. Life during the umbrella factory era had been bliss. Throngs of people meant plenty of food for them to eat, always an open window to attract good, meaty, fly dinners and lots of healthy plants to play in. After the fire, nothing was left. Many spiders had died. Those who survived hid their pain as best they could, crawling on the rafters day in and day out, scrounging for whatever scraps they could find. Things seemed hopeless. Generations of spiders worked hard to establish themselves at the umbrella factory. It was their territory. After the catastrophe, it was too late to regroup anywhere else. Every building in the city already had its own colony. New members were never allowed. A strict spider rule. Octavian the First grew weary seeing his family and friends fall into the depths of despair. Depression was wide spread. Food had to be rationed. Tempers flared. But he somehow kept everyone together.

After he and his wife bore a mere four hundred children, they created a new and improved colony for everyone. Their lives were enriched when Factory founder, Lulu, and the Sticks took over. The spiders once again had hope. The cats provided them with a source of nourishment and adventure, though the cats didn't know it. Of course, there was always that one fearless spider sneaking up on Sticks trying to impress his friends. Once in a while he'd get away with a little taste of blood, but most of the time he'd fall into the jaws of doom. Not the most enticing way to go, down the furballed pipes of a smelly cat. Nevertheless, Octavian IV and his family were the current leaders of the S.S., better known as the Spider Society. In fact, Octavian and some of his brothers were presently installing a new park on the top floor that promised to be a big success. Named the Fly Zone, it featured such things as fly legs on a stick, fly slides made from actual wings, a web maze, and the twelve-legged race. Octavian IV was well on his way to becoming a legend.

It was eight A.M. and most of the Alley cats were still passed out from a long night of partying. Smelly's would be opening soon for the early risers, the losers that need a drink first thing in the morning. Fidel had been one of those.

Bait, Cheeseburger, and Irving woke with pounding headaches. Dehydrated and tired, Bait barely remembered his evening at the Glitteroom. As for Cheeseburger, the flashbacks were already setting in. And then there was Irving. Poor Irving had two deaths under his paisley belt, and he hadn't even been in town for one full day.

Cheeseburger began to hunt for breakfast. A good wholesome meal was just what he needed to settle his stomach. He looked through every garbage bin and trash heap in the alley. There was nothing left. He walked over to Bait who was cleaning the morning sludge between his toes with his teeth. "What's to eats around dis place?" Cheeseburger growled. "I'm hungry!" When Cheeseburger was hungry, watch out! Cranky did not begin to explain him. One time he actually nibbled off the tip of Bait's tail. Bait whacked him with a shoe filled with mud. The bump was still there.

"I don't know," Bait cried. "Ain't there any of dat mousy left? He was purdy tasty!" Bait rubbed his paws together and laughed making a snorting sound.

"Hey," Cheeseburger whispered in Bait's ear with a sudden idea. "Why don't we make da new guy gets us somethin'? So far he's done nothin' around here but die. Whadaya say, Bait?"

"Boss! Call me boss!" Bait insisted, power welling up inside of him.

Cheeseburger gurgled up a furball. "You ain't my boss!"

Bait puffed out his scrawny, little chest and took in a long, deep breath. He tried to look tough, and almost did, until he began to cough uncontrollably. "As long as Fidel's not around, I'm in charge, see?" he snapped. "Haven't you learned that by now? It's only been like two years!"

Cheeseburger drooled onto the ground with a dazed look on his face. "Whatever! Anyhoo, whadaya say we send Fancy Pants for take out?"

"Well, he did say he wanted to work," Bait said with a wicked little laugh. "We could sleep whiles he goes out! I could use some more shut-eye. What's your poison? Fish? Birds? Sticks?"

Cheeseburger rolled on his back in laughter. He was easily amused. Bait went back to his pedicure, making sure to dig up even the oldest crud. Soon Irving started his morning rituals too.

"What's he doin'?" Bait pointed with his toe sticking from his mouth. Cheeseburger twisted his head around and immediately stopped his laughing to see Irving in his morning yoga routine. To the hum of his droning purr, he stretched and arched and twisted himself into all sorts of unnatural positions. Cheeseburger tried to follow Irving's serpentine body with his gaze, but became completely cross-eyed. Irving tilted his head back and let out a long, "Ummmmm." It was freaky.

"Getta load of the rubber cat!" Bait howled.

"I tink he's dancin'!" Cheeseburger wailed.

Irving was in a deep trance and completely unaware of his hecklers. He went on with his nature ballet until something knocked him in the head. It was an old, wormy apple core that Bait had thrown.

"I do say!" Irving bumbled, rubbing the sore spot on his head. "What is the meaning of this?" He untangled his body and blew out his three scented candles.

"Tee-hee-hee!" Cheeseburger laughed. "He gotcha, Fancy Pants!"

"Listen, you two hooligans," Irving began, "if you think I'm going to put up with your shenanigans, then you've got another thing coming!" He kicked the apple out of his way. "And another thing, I am hardly amused by the

Chapter Six

insensitive little alias you think is so comical."

"Huh?" Bait asked, never having heard such hoity-toity language. Remember, not only was he a street cat, but he was also one of the dumbest.

Cheeseburger thought real hard. "I think he means you farted."

Irving sat back down and began to make his bed. "What I meant was, my name is Irving! I would appreciate you addressing me only as that."

"I don't wear no dresses, but if you want me to call you Irving, Irving it'll be...even though it's a sissy name," Bait cracked.

"And furthermore, I have hardly been here more than a day and I have already lost two lives!" Irving snapped, still in a bit of shock over the entire situation. "Can you believe that? Two lives! Dreadful! Simply dreadful!"

Bait really didn't care about his two lives. He was just hungry. Cheeseburger, too. In fact, Cheeseburger's tummy was beginning to growl. Then Bait remembered their plan. "Tell ya what, Fancy Pants...I mean, Irving," Bait began. Sauntering over, he put his paw to Irving's shoulder. "We's all hungry around here, and my head's killing me!"

"I'm hungry! I'm hungry!" Cheeseburger wailed as he jumped up and down, rattling the entire alleyway.

"I bet you're hungry, too," Bait suggested. "Ain't ya?" Bait ran his tongue along his plaque covered teeth and smiled big.

Life Four

Irving looked at both of them suspiciously. "Yes," he began. "I could use a nibble or two of some delicious cakes."

Sneaky Bait reached his back paw behind him and crossed his toes. "Down by da wharf there's loads a fishies and stuffs to eats. Whadaya say you go down there and grab us some grub? And to make up for last night and dis morning, we'll have da place all tidied up and...pretty for when you come back! Just the way you likes it. Like your old home."

Irving thought about this, while Bait and Cheeseburger watched with swirly eyes and grumbling tummies. A little feel of home sounded good. Yearning for a walk in the city and a chance to get away from the two bozos, Irving agreed. "Oh, all right, tell me where I might find les poisons."

Bait and Cheeseburger looked at each other with sneaky grins.

Irving glanced back at his private, dusty corner. "Please promise you will be careful with my belongings. I have many important things, and they mustn't be disturbed."

Bait lifted his chin as high as it would go. "You gots my word," he said, his toes still crossed behind his back.

As soon as Irving had his instructions, he was off. Bait and Cheeseburger burst into villainous laughter, pummeling each other with high fives. Five minutes later they were back asleep, passed out on the alley floor.

Chapter Six

Irving had a mission. Find breakfast. He was on this journey without his favorite pants. Bait thought it best. Irving loved those silk, paisley, fancy pants. Still, he stepped out into the crisp, morning air. The sun was trying desperately to chisel its way through the thick mortar of clouds, but the cool breeze did him good. It somehow soothed his aching head.

Irving walked proudly down the streets of his new city. Looking up and down the tall skyscrapers, he marveled at their unique construction and old world charm, something most cats never noticed or even knew about.

By the time Irving reached the city dock, the old church bells chimed nine. Some people lived their whole lives by those chimes. Time to get up. Time to go to work. Time to go home. But lately, the bell tower lady was getting lazy. Some days she never even bothered showing up.

At the dock Irving breathed in the fine fish air, the kind that would make most humans puke. Immediately, he recognized the small boat he had sailed on when coming to this new and grand land. He wondered if he was missed back home.

Directly in Irving's view was the island Romeo and his friends had been marooned on two years earlier. Because of the morning fog, he could only see the statue from its knees down. But still, he knew hidden up in those misty clouds was a goddess. A symbol. An emblem for this new place he called home.

Life Four

Just as Bait had said, down the far left side of the dock were several smaller boats. Fishing boats. Short, beefy men in yellow plastic overalls and little funny hats scrambled around pulling ropes and gathering nets. They were already well into their busy day. From where he stood, Irving could see several buckets in the boats. *The fish must be in those!* Irving said to himself. Although Bait explained how he should bring the fish back, Irving doubted that strapping them to his paws would really work. So, he decided to do things his way.

First, he had to stake out the place, find out which buckets contained what, which fishermen to watch, and decide how much fish he could steal and carry back to the alley. After doing an initial inspection, using very careful spy-like techniques, Irving had a plan. He would wait until the fishermen went inside their little shack, which they seemed to do every few minutes or so, and then go in for the kill. Under a plank, Irving found a small, though sturdy plastic bag. He would fill it with the yummiest fish he could grab and bolt out of there like pure hell. If he was lucky, he wouldn't find any trouble along the way. But in a city like this, there was always that possibility.

On his tippy toes, Irving snuck up to the closest boat. It was tied to the dock with a thick, braided rope. Printed on the boat's side were the words, Fat Joe. Nobody was on it. Perfect. The men were in their shack.

He eyed the bucket of fish sitting smack

dab in the middle of the deck. With the plastic bag clutched tightly in his teeth, he sunk to a low prowl and slithered in. As he did, the boat rocked and rolled against the water. Some of the fish spilled out of their bucket. Icky juice gushed everywhere. "Oh, goody! Soup!" Irving said with tantalizing delight.

"Go get the rest, Jack!" one of the fisherman suddenly shouted. "There's another load on Fat Joe's."

When Irving heard that, he knew he hadn't a moment to spare. He must hide fast! Without thinking, Irving dove into the fish bucket and hid under a plump mackerel. He tugged frantically at its puffy lips trying to cover himself. His back paws crunched down on another fish, scooping its eyes out like ice cream. "Oh, my goodness!" Irving wailed under five pounds of deliciously slimy scales. He was hiding in his own private Nirvana.

Just then, Lazy Jack, one of the fishermen, pulled the boat closer to the dock. "Take these fish," Jack called out to Joe. Irving could feel his bucket being lifted.

"Trow dat bucket over here!" cried Joe from an even bigger bucket of fish. In fact, it was more like a tank. "Put 'em in with these guys."

Irving tightly grabbed two fish fins. His paws kept sliding off, though he was determined. Lazy Jack dumped the whole load from the bucket into the huge bin of fish. Plop! Plop! Plop! Irving went sailing out with the rest of the fish. The fins finally slipped right out of his clutches tossing Irving down deeper into the stink. One gaping, open-mouthed mackerel wrapped its huge, fat lips around Irving's face. Even a fish-loving cat didn't like this. Gross!

Lazy Jack hadn't seen Irving fall in, but he did notice something strange. "Hey, Joe!" he called.

"What is it?"

"Der's something fishy about these fish!"

"What is it?" Joe asked again, enjoying his third jelly donut of the morning.

"I think some are still alive!" Lazy Jack shouted. "They're moving!"

Joe came running outside with grape goo all over his chin. "Awe, that's impossible, Jack," he said. "They've been outta the water a long time. You've been sniffin' them again, haven't you?"

Jack stared at the ground. "Look, forget about that. Them fish is moving! Take a look for yourself!"

Joe stood over the bin. It was filled to the brim with fish. Lots of fish. Nothing was moving. "You're crazy!" he said. "You just thought..."

But then, Irving felt pointy fins sliding toward his butt. He flailed his paws violently trying to push the fish away.

"They is moving!" Joe shouted. "Dat's impossible!" He rushed off in a hurry.

"Where you going?" Lazy Jack yelled.

In seconds, Joe came running out of the shack holding a large baseball bat. "I'm gonna kill

Chapter Six

them fishies!" he howled with the bat raised high over his head. "Look out below!"

With a loud whack Joe thrust the bat savagely into the fish bin, swinging again and again, slicing and dicing the fish into tiny bits. Fish parts exploded all over him. Fish heads, tails, and fins. Somewhere in all that mess Irving innocently scurried around in horror.

"One's still alive!" Jack roared. "I saw it jump!"

Joe held the bat even higher, fish guts stuck to him. His eyes burned with anger. "Take this!" he cried. "Wait a minute! Fishies don't have pointy ears and fur!"

Joe and Lazy Jack looked closely into the gruesome pit of fishy mush and for the first time saw Irving. "A cat's in there!" Jack shouted. Joe stuck his hand into the mess making gurgling, burpy noises with the fish guts. He pulled Irving out by the collar.

"You're right, Jack!" Joe said with surprise, holding a very limp Irving up to his face. "What do I do with him? He's dead!"

Joe was right. Irving was dead all right. That final smack did him in. His head was hit hard with the bat. Not an easy way to go.

"Awe, just trow him in the water," Lazy Jack suggested.

With that, Irving was thrown ten feet into the air like a frisbee. Joe and Jack watched him sail down, down into the water with a splash. "Yeah!!"

they hollered, high fiving each other with bloody, fish hands.

"Come on," Jack began, "we needs to clean up this mess." So the two fishermen went back to their work with diligent efficiency as Irving's lifeless body floated in the harbor.

Romeo managed to escape another one of his father's lectures by bolting out the door. After about an hour, he found himself on Dennis's corner for the first time in nearly two years. He had avoided it like the plague. It was just too painful.

He sat down on the cold sidewalk and walked his eyes up the five flights of red bricks as a tight knot welled up in his throat. The building seemed taller and bigger than he had remembered, towering like a statue.

Spotting Dennis's window, a flood of memories and warm sensations came gushing forward. He could almost smell Dennis's room, imagine the walls, and taste the fresh canned food. It was still a part of him. He fondly remembered his first meeting with Dennis. Dennis's tenth birthday. A happy time. Mr. Crumb sneaked little Romeo into the apartment in a tiny, cardboard box. When Dennis opened the box, cat and boy looked at each other and knew they'd be the best of friends forever. But that was a long time ago. Dennis was almost thirteen now and miles away from that long gone day. And here was where it all began. Home. A happy, safe place when the rest of

Chapter Six

the world was frightening and dangerous. Now that wonderful feeling of belonging was gone. He didn't belong there any longer. He didn't belong anywhere.

In a rush decision, Romeo found himself climbing the old, familiar vine up to the fifth floor. He remembered the route immediately. Down below, the people got smaller and smaller until they looked like little bugs.

When Romeo reached the branch outside Dennis's window, he crawled carefully on, getting as close as he could. He was very quiet. He had to be. If Dennis saw him, he'd be totally spooked. After all, Dennis believed Romeo had died at the vet's office. He instinctively turned towards Gwen's room across the alley where Queen Elizabeth had lived and where Twinkle Toes now lived. Romeo missed Queen Elizabeth so much. So much, in fact, he had to look away.

To Romeo's surprise Dennis's window was open. Although Dennis preferred keeping his window closed, he kept it open when Romeo lived there so he could come and go as he pleased. But why was it open now? Did Dennis have another cat?

Romeo cautiously peered inside. His heart started to swell. His lips became dry. It was early Saturday morning, and he knew Dennis would be there.

Romeo looked with tear filled eyes at the desk, over the scattered toys and magazines, and

Life Four

all the way to the bed. There, on new superhero sheets, was Dennis. *I bet he forgot all about me*, Romeo sighed to himself. Dennis was asleep, and although he was pretty tied up in his blankets, Romeo was able to get a good look at him. He looked different. Dennis had grown up. His feet reached the end of the bed, his face had changed, and his body was oddly bigger. For a brief moment, Romeo forgot where he was and what he was doing. He felt as if he had never left. But reality always had a way of slapping him back to his senses.

As Romeo snapped out of his trance, he noticed Pierre the poodle curled up in a tiny ball on the opposite pillow. Even though Pierre did come to Romeo's aid at the revolt two years ago, Romeo still wanted to dislike him. But deep down Romeo knew he wasn't such a bad guy. He'd seen his true colors that fateful day. Still, nothing changed the fact that Romeo was insanely jealous of Pierre. After all, Romeo didn't get to sleep on that pillow anymore.

On the bedside table, Romeo saw the empty spot where his picture once stood, the one the rats had stolen. He then noticed three things he had never seen in Dennis's room before. A pair of glasses, a retainer, and something even more unexpected. Romeo squinted hard. *My collar! He saved it!* He yelled in his mind. Romeo was overcome by a tingling sense of joy. *He hasn't forgotten me!*

Just then, as Romeo was feeling alive for the

first time in two years, a startling sound caught his attention. Leaves rattled, branches shook, someone else was in his tree. Pierre woke up out of his sleep, and Romeo could swear he looked right at him. Quickly, Romeo climbed farther and farther down the tree to the vines and over the awning below. In a flash, he ran toward the Factory. Little did he know a long rat's tail slithered sinisterly into Dennis's room. Another followed closely behind. Pierre's eyes widened.

Romeo ran all the way back to the Factory with determination in his gut. He had to get that food for the rats. He simply had to. Nothing would stop him now. He wouldn't let them hurt Dennis. He burst into the Factory zipping by Waffles, knocking over Vittles. "Outta my way!" he cried. "Move it!" Vittles dusted himself off with a look of pure disgust.

"Whatever," Vittles snapped.

Inside, everyone was busy putting the finishing touches on the Factory's big opening ceremony. Darla and Tabitha were hanging last minute decorations. Fluffy and Mr. Shadow were dusting the shelves, and a pawful of others swept and scrubbed. Snickers and Uncle Fred attempted to look busy by wandering around in circles, although they were actually doing nothing at all, just waiting for breakfast to be served. But somebody was missing. Where was Calvin?

"Wasn't he supposed to be here?" Darla asked in Tabitha's direction.

Chapter Six

"He said he'd be here," Tabitha replied. "I wonder where he could be."

On the other side of town Calvin was leading his very own stakeout. He heard about Flannigan's escape from City Jail on Lloyd's television. There was no doubt in Calvin's self-centered mind that he was, in fact, number one on Buggles's target list. After all, he was the one who got Buggles arrested. Buggles had been committing crimes around the city for years, stealing, bank robbing. He'd done it all, but Calvin got him caught, that was for sure.

Calvin crept cautiously through the city. Buggles could be anywhere, he thought to himself. He could be stalking me at this very moment! Bubastis! Still, he had to do what he had to do. It was his job. His very survival depended on it.

When he finally reached Buggles's building, a familiar nausea swirled in his belly. He'd never forget that building. It was pathetic. Your average, everyday flop house, worn and neglected. The front entrance had two large, wooden doors, each with nasty graffiti etched around the sides amongst other gashes and carvings. Inside wasn't any better. Misfits, mostly addicts, alcoholics, dropouts, or in Buggles's case, cat-nappers. A swarm of sunken eyed, rotten-toothed junkies patrolled the third floor. Several of the city's most senile were often seen leaning out of the fourth floor windows or just talking to themselves out front. Buggles himself hadn't been around the place for the two years he was jailed, but his brother Chip had been seen freeloading off his 'estate'. Calvin carefully checked his reflection in Jake's Apple and Gun Shop and headed for the front door, a cold sweat bursting from deep inside him.

Determined, Calvin began the short climb up to Buggles's window. Remembering that dirty, cramped apartment he was held hostage in almost made him gag, but he kept going. He shimmied up a dangling clothesline like a circus performer.

Buggles's window was cloudy and spotted and draped with putrid looking orange, cigarette burned curtains. Calvin was able to see in through a small spot. Just as he suspected, there was Buggles sitting on his same crummy couch, scraping off the same junk from his remaining teeth.

"Hey, Chip! Whadaya got for breakfast?" Buggles snapped at his brother, a toothpick stuck between his two front teeth. "I'm starved!"

Calvin could hear some serious noise over near the tiny kitchen window. A pan fell, the water ran on and off, and something was apparently lodged in the disposal. "We got two onions and five...no, one can a lima beans. What'll it be? I know what I want." Chip began chopping the onions. Raw onion was his favorite meal. As he hacked away with the only utensil they had, a long, wooden pencil, tears trickled down his cratered cheeks.

"Onions and beans?" Buggles roared from the couch. "No eggs? What about some eggs?"

Chapter Six

Chip, wearing a smashing plaid apron, wiped the tears from his burning eyes. "We ain't got no eggs, Bugs! You threw 'em all out the winder at that bird! Don't you remember? Now, come on in here and have some onions. I'm cuttin' them into little bitty pieces! Just like you like!"

Buggles clenched his angry fists so tightly, his nails dug through the stuffing of the sofa. "All right, all right," he mumbled. "Just make it quick! I got stuff to do."

Still outside, Calvin listened closely to Buggles's voice. It was a voice he hoped he'd never hear again. But here he was trying to find out what Buggles was up to. He had to protect himself anyway possible.

Buggles and his brother continued to bicker until Buggles finally had enough. "Forget the onions! Get me a newspaper!" he hollered. "I need something to burn!"

"Awe relax, Bugs!" Chip whined with eyes full of onion tears. "Why don't you go back and sit down. When I finish my onions, we can get your paper and..."

"Now!" Buggles roared. "Or the plan is off!"

Calvin's ears perked up.

"All right, all right. I'll get the stupid paper," Chip said dropping the pencil to the floor. "I'll be right back, okay? You just wait here. Don't leave without me. I wouldn't wanna miss out on all the fun."

Fun? Calvin wondered with intense

Life Four

curiosity. What fun?

Buggles stood tight with his shoulders practically up to his ears. His fists clenched, and his eyes squinted. When he wanted something, he got it. Chip had no choice.

Chip raced out the door and headed for the nearest market. Of course, he was going to steal the paper, and maybe an egg or two. Buggles had taught him how to do it. Nobody in the Flannigan family ever paid for anything. That was their legacy.

A plan, huh! Calvin leaned back and thought. It must have something to do with me. I knew something was up!

With that, Calvin climbed down in a flash, knowing he'd soon be back to find out more. But first he had to tell everyone at the Factory that Buggles and Chip were up to something. Something bad. Calvin would need help.

Romeo paced nervously outside the basement door. He had to get back down there and snatch one of those dog collars to bring to Trixie. But what if he got caught? What would everyone say? His father would never understand. Not this time. So what! He didn't care what anyone thought. Romeo continued to walk back and forth awaiting the right moment to strike.

"Breakfast break!" Roy and Yellowtail called from behind a large tin of Smuggler's Salty Cat Food. "Dig in!" Despite the city's hardships, Roy and Yellowtail still had access to their favorite fish

Chapter Six

market. For a while, fresh fish was hard to come by due to the long strike. But since the dispute was settled, Roy and Yellowtail once again had free reign of the fish scraps and even managed to up their supply of cat food. Their person became so busy at the shop, he was feeding them double and didn't even realize it. They brought the extra food to the Factory like the loyal and generous Sticks that they were.

"Oh, yummy!" Uncle Fred roared. He could smell those morsels from across the room. "I get first dibs!"

"Oh no, you don't!" Snickers yelled, bolting over to the dish. "I've been waiting just as long as you!"

Foreseeing disaster, Mr. Sox intervened. "Males! Males!" he said in a fatherly tone. "There's enough for everyone. Why don't you..."

But it was too late. Uncle Fred and Snickers had already managed to destroy the entire supply. They grappled each other like two mud wrestlers at a championship match. Chunks of meaty goodness flew everywhere, smacking other Sticks and smashing against the walls. Covered from head to paw in guts, Fred and Snickers flopped to the floor out of breath and embarrassed.

"What have you done?" Roy screamed. "You've ruined my breakfast!"

"You idiots!" Yellowtail sneered.

From the back of the room Twinkle Toes was busy licking the food off the wall. "It's cool,

Life Four

dudes," he said between licks. "It's still good, just a little messy."

Soon everyone joined him for a little taste of wall, giving Romeo the chance to finally sneak down into the basement unnoticed. He had to keep track of the time. Mr. Gamble had just left for his morning power walk with Tuesday, Delio, and Mr. Shadow. They would be back in an hour. Carefully sticking his paw under the door, Romeo was just about to pull it open when he heard a voice.

"What are you doing, Romeo?" Candle asked, standing behind him, her red fur arranged nicely on her head. "You're not going down there, are you?"

"Beat it, Candle," Romeo snapped. "Scram!" As Romeo turned away, he heard Candle begin to sniffle. She sat down on her little bottom with her head to the floor as the tears poured out. Romeo rolled his eyes and clicked his tongue against his teeth. "Awe, come on, Candle," he whined. "Quit your blubbering!"

Candle looked up with her sad eyes. "Oh, Romeo!" she cried. "Why can't you just...? Why?" She raced to the other side of the room with tears streaming down her face. She didn't know what else to do.

Romeo watched her go with little care. He was too focused on getting one of those collars out of the yucky pile of bones. He wasn't leaving without it.

Again, Romeo slipped his paw under the

Chapter Six

basement door and pulled. This time, no surprises. He carefully crept around the door and closed it quietly. Now inside, Romeo took in a deep breath and looked down the long flight of stairs. It was as dark and silent as it had been before. No sign of Octavian.

Romeo headed straight for what he thought was the bone room. He looked down with a flinch and saw the piles of old papers. The same papers he'd found earlier. *This isn't it*, he said with a scrunched face feeling something jabbing his foot. There on the floor between his toes was that forgotten picture drawn by the young Queen Elizabeth. Romeo kicked it out of his way. *Now, where are those bones?*

After a short search, Romeo found the small room. Cobwebs dripped from the ceiling and a chalky dust lingered in the air like summer mosquitoes. A pinch of sunlight poked through the same cracked window illuminating the room just enough. Cat bones, dog bones, bird bones, all swarming with maggots. *Cool*, Romeo thought. *I found them! Leg bones, tail bones, jaws and teeth.* Romeo didn't dwell on the morbidity of the situation. He was too excited to be concerned with a pile of dead guys. As he rummaged through the stack, he came across some of the old, forgotten collars. *One of these has got to be a dog's collar. It's got to be!*

Ah-ha! Romeo cried, holding a shiny piece of gold. *This is a dog's!* On the thick leather strap dangled a small golden rectangle. Spot, it said in engraved letters. Only a dog would be named Spot, Romeo decided with a sinister grin.

Romeo bolted out of the basement like a bandit, the collar dangling loosely from his neck. He ran through the rec room, racing for the front door while the others were licking their paws clean of their tasty breakfast. Candle watched Romeo as he dashed down the street, her tiny nose sticking out into the air through a window. "What are you up to, Romeo?" she whispered to herself. And she followed him.

Back in the alley, Bait and Cheeseburger anxiously awaited their morning fish. "Do you think he can really do it, Bait?" Cheeseburger asked sitting up tall and donning a stained, old bandana as a bib. "Do you think Irving will bring us the fishies?"

"Boss! Call me boss!" Bait screeched.

Cheeseburger gave him that same funny look. "Really though, do you think he'll make it? I'm starvin' here!" he whined.

Bait paced around in the alley, stabbing his toe on a tack. "He'd better bring us dose fishies or I'll...I'll...I'll be really mad!" he scowled.

"Maybe I'll go looks for him," Cheeseburger said, prancing over to the street. "I'm bored."

"No!" Bait wailed suddenly in a violent shiver. "Stay here! Don't go nowheres. I uh... think you should stay in da alley. Remember da big rats!"

Chapter Six

Cheeseburger came back and looked at Bait with new curiosity. "Hey, are you chicken...Bait, I mean, boss?" he began, cackling like a chicken. "You're not scared of them rats, are you? Cats can take rats any day! Bok! Bok! Bok!"

"Stop it!" Bait whined. "Why would I be scared of a bunch a rats? Huh?" Bait clenched his teeth together and shivered. "I'm just weak from hunger. Yeah, dat's it! Where's our breakfast already?"

But Cheeseburger didn't believe him. Still, as he waited for Irving's return, Cheeseburger spent much of the morning being Bait's shadow, leaping and running around in dizzying circles. To Bait's delight, Cheeseburger eventually fell asleep from sheer exhaustion. Bait just stared down the street...waiting.

Chapter Seven

Romeo wasn't sure where that old school yard was, but he figured his personal taxi would be along any minute to take him there. Unnerving as it was, he was beginning to rely on it. But as more time passed, Romeo began to wonder if the cab would come at all.

It was almost ten o'clock in the morning, and once again Romeo was lost, painfully lost. He was very far from the Factory, this he knew. But where? Romeo didn't even recognize any of the words on the buildings. They weren't made up of the letters he knew. They were like funny little pictures. Even the passing feet seemed to speak a different language. Just as he was about to sprint ahead, Romeo heard a noise coming from behind the newspaper rack near the curb. He could see the tips of someone's wet paws. "Who's that?" he said quickly turning on his Alley radar. Romeo squinted hard. "Look, I don't want any trouble." On tippy-toes, Romeo inched closer. As he did, he suddenly saw a small tuft of red fur. Immediately, he knew exactly who it was. "Candle?" he hollered. "Is that you under there?"

From behind the big newspaper rack, a little pink nose stuck out. "Romeo?" her tiny voice said. "What are you doing in China Town?"

Romeo flapped his tail in the air and walked over to her. Having someone know his business was not what he needed now. Especially Candle. "You're going to get hurt! You better get back to the Factory!" he scolded taking in a deep sigh of anger.

Candle tried to look confident, but her voice was weak and nervous. "I can take care of myself," she boasted.

Romeo paced back and forth. "Look, go back and don't tell anyone you saw me," he insisted. "I don't have time to explain. It's too complicated." But Candle just stood there defiant. "Please, just go home," he pleaded. "Okay? I need to do...something."

"Romeo, why are you wearing that huge collar around your neck?" she asked having completely disregarded everything he had just said. "That's not yours, is it? Now, would you please tell me what's going on? I'm worried about you."

Life Four

Romeo realized he had to say something or she wasn't going away. "Look, I need to take this to the second corner. It's something I just gotta do," he explained quickly looking everywhere but into her eyes.

"Huh?" Candle exploded with a sudden gasp. "The second corner? Are you crazy? Don't you know that place...," she lowered her voice, "is haunted?"

"Haunted? What are you talking about?"

"Haven't you ever heard of the phantom school yard?" Candle asked.

Romeo thought about the spooky school yard and the subway train that came barreling out of nowhere. He could still hear the eerie laughter even now. "You must be crazy," he snapped, shaking the memory from his head. "There's no such thing as a phantom school."

Candle looked at him wide-eyed. "Sure there is! Everyone knows about it. At least, all us Alleys do," she said with a pinch of shame. "Ever since those kids disappeared at that school, the whole block has been haunted! That's why the second corner is such a scary place! Nobody wants to go down there! Nobody!"

"How do you know about the school yard?" Romeo asked with an urgency to his voice.

Candle rolled her eyes at him. "How many times do I have to tell you, Romeo? I'm an Alley! Remember? We know about these things! And we know to stay away!"

Chapter Seven

"Yeah? Well, I've already been down there and I didn't see any..."

"What?" Candle shrieked. "You've been down there? You've got to be kidding, Romeo! Tell me you didn't go!"

"What's the big deal, Candle?" Romeo asked as he wiggled his paw around in little circles. "Nothing happened."

A chill shot up Candle's entire body. After everything she heard, could this be true? Did Romeo actually go to the second corner and live to tell about it? "You didn't lose...a life, did you?" she finally asked. "Because they say nobody comes out alive! At least, they don't come out with the same amount of lives they go in with."

"No, way! Nothing like that happened," Romeo explained. "Look, I need to get this dog collar down there so this Trixie chick can help me take care of another...problem. It's very complicated. The thing is, I don't remember where the place is."

Candle looked out into the morning and watched as some children chased each other down the street with brooms. It was easy to forget the cats shared the city with two million people. "I can take you there. I know where it is."

"Are you sure?"

"I'm an Alley, remember?" she said again with great emphasis. "I know this city, I already told you that."

Romeo thought it over. He liked the idea

of her going along, but at the same time he didn't want to explain the whole sordid story. She might tell his father. Then again, he would need her help later getting the food to Hog. But should he tell her about the taxi? Or the bones? Nah, she'd think he was nuts. Romeo stared at her innocent face and knew he had to take a chance. At this point, having a turncoat in his corner might just be what he needed. He knew he could trust her. She had always been good to him, even when he didn't deserve it.

"All right, you can come with," he agreed after some serious considering, "but I don't want to tell you everything I know, not yet."

"No problem," Candle reassured with a hearty smile. "Just follow me."

Candle was right. She did know the way. She led Romeo down eight long blocks to the old, abandoned schoolhouse. As soon as he laid his eyes on that broken down building and the melted jungle gym, he knew he was where he needed to be.

"I've gotta hand it to you, Candle," Romeo said as he stood looking out at the murky playground. "You do know your city."

Candle stepped back and smiled. "But now, about that second corner. You've really been in there?" she asked nervously.

"Yes, yes I have."

"I don't know, Romeo. Are you sure you should chance it again?" Candle asked with a quiver in her voice. "What if this time something...

Chapter Seven

happens? I mean, it was probably just a fluke that you made it out before!"

"It wasn't, Candle!" With the collar dangling from his neck, Romeo bolted forward and headed for the subway station. "I'm going! I've got to!"

As much as Candle wanted to help, and as much as she liked Romeo, she couldn't go beyond this point. She would wait in front of the corroded playground equipment, keeping a close eye out for anything suspicious until he came back.

Romeo ran all the way down to the train tracks. Like before, the place was deserted. The same garbage, the same smell, even the same bugs. *The vent*, he thought with his eyes swirling in his head. *There's the vent*. Romeo leaped over the subway tracks. He was on a mission.

After crawling through the vent and spotting the stone bats, Romeo found his way back to Trixie's cavern. Once inside, he waited in the cold darkness.

After what seemed like hours, a large rock suddenly moved. Like an earthquake, the cave rattled and shook, dust flying all around. Then, out of a smoky cloud, Trixie emerged on her metal pipe, all four wings and everything. Marlow was standing behind her. Trixie took a long, slow look at Romeo.

"You have returned," she said in a low monotone. "Did you bring me a collar?"

"Yes, yes, I did," Romeo mumbled. With his front paw, he reached around his neck and

Chapter Seven

slipped it off his head. "Here...here's your collar." Romeo dropped it on the cold, hard floor.

"Bring it here," Trixie moaned. "Give it to Marlow."

Slow and steady, Romeo walked to Marlow with the collar in his teeth. Again, he put it on the floor.

Marlow brought the collar to Trixie. She examined it carefully. Then after a long silence, she spoke. "Well done, young Romeo." She turned to Marlow. "Put the collar in my safe." Marlow retreated into another room where he placed the collar with Trixie's other 'treasures', including four human toes, two snake tongues, one prehistoric egg, and several other exotic possessions. After a few moments, Marlow re-emerged. "Good," Trixie said. She turned to Romeo. "Now, on to our business. What is it you came for? Why did Hog send you to me?"

Romeo remembered what the rats told him. Trixie likes Hog. As a bat, she felt connected to the rat population. But then again, Candle warned Romeo of her evil side. "Hog wants food," Romeo said slowly.

"Food? Food?" Trixie eyed him sternly. "What has that got to do with me? Hmm?"

Romeo explained the whole situation as quickly as he could. The rats, the catering table, Dennis. "...and I have to pick up the first batch by seven tomorrow morning or it will be too late! The rats are starving to death since the revolt, and

112

it's all my fault, but I don't know what to do!"

Trixie stared at him as he told his sad tale. When he finished, she turned her back and began to chant. "Zee-zee! Da-da!" Romeo didn't understand what she was doing. Still, he listened. Marlow stood like a soldier. "Here's what you must do," Trixie finally announced.

"Yes!" Romeo said with excitement.

Trixie closed her eyes and concentrated. "I see a taxi following you, am I right?"

"Yes! Yes! But how did you...."

"Silence!" she shrieked. "This taxi, you must find it again." As she spoke she drew her ugly head nearer and nearer to Romeo.

"But how?" Romeo asked.

"I said silence!" Trixie swung back and forth on the pipe. "Zee-zee! Da-da! Find the taxi. Put the food inside. The taxi will drive you to the rats. Zee-zee. That is what you must do." Trixie finished and curled her body under her wings. She and Marlow began to dissolve into the darkness.

"Wait!" Romeo cried. "Where's the cab? Does he know what to do? Please come back!"

But it was too late. Trixie and Marlow were gone. Romeo stood alone and scared.

Romeo roamed the vacant passageways until he finally found his way back to the vent. He squeezed through the slats and raced outside. Candle was waiting right where he'd left her.

"There you are!" she hollered from the misty schoolyard as she raced towards him. "You're all right! Tell me what happened!"

Romeo ran right past her at Olympic speed. "I've got no time to explain! I've got to find that cab!" He zigzagged through the empty street and back around again. He lost precious time in that bat pit, and there was no more left to lose now.

"Cab? What cab?" Candle yelled, trying to keep up. "Did you meet with that lady? What did she say? Did she take the collar?"

"Candle, you can't stay!" Romeo shouted. "I think the taxi only finds me when I'm alone! You've got to go! Now!"

"Romeo, what are you talking about?" Candle cried. "You're not making any sense!"

"Please, Candle!" Romeo roared with intensity in his eyes. Though he could have used a friend, it was too risky to keep her around.

Candle threw her head back and dashed around the corner as Romeo paraded through the streets. However, she watched him from behind a fallen newspaper rack as he ran in maniacal circles hoping the elusive cab would spot him. It was terrible. The swirl in his eyes and drool from his mouth made Candle wonder if he was on the nip.

For another hour, this macabre circus continued. Romeo seemed more desperate than ever. Candle wouldn't leave him. Not until she had some answers. But she'd stay out of sight.

And then it happened. A dingy, yellow cab came thumping up the street. Romeo recognized the rumble of that lazy engine. He began to pant

Life Four

heavily. *There it is!* he cried to himself. *He came! I knew he would!* Romeo ran into the street waving his tail like mad. His body was covered in a slick layer of sheen from the perspiration. "Over here!" he squealed. "I'm over here!" But the cab just kept on driving down the street. Romeo ran after it for as long as he could, but it was no use. The taxi was gone. Out of breath, Romeo collapsed to the cold concrete. Candle immediately came running to his aid.

"Romeo! Romeo, are you okay?" she screamed cupping him in her paws. Romeo was passed out from exhaustion. He lay limp in Candle's lap as she frantically shook him awake. "Wake up! Wake up!" She began to slap him across his face. And then, just when she was about to drag him away and yell for help, Romeo spoke.

"What happened?" he grumbled, his eyelids quivering.

"You're okay!" Candle cried. "You're going to be all right!"

Romeo looked up from his daze past her pretty eyes and up into the afternoon sky. "Did he get away?" he cried as he squirmed to his feet. "Didn't you stop him? Don't let him get away!" Romeo collapsed right back down and waved his paw in the air.

"What are you talking about, Romeo?" Candle held him tightly around his middle to keep him from escaping. "Don't let who get away?"

"The cab! Didn't you see the cab?"

Chapter Seven

"What cab?" Candle asked, zipping her head nervously around. "There's no cab here!"

Candle knew there was no cab in sight and was resigned to finding out the truth. She had a fire in her eyes and a passion in her voice. "I'm not leaving until you tell me what's going on! I mean it!"

Romeo was confused. This was a side of Candle he never knew existed. With a dramatic sigh, Romeo gave in. "Oh, all right," he said weakly. "I'll tell you...everything, but you have to promise not to tell anyone! Not a soul!"

"Promise!" Candle agreed.

Over at the wharf, Irving's dead body floated quietly in the open water as Joe and Lazy Jack took a much needed break from their grisly morning of work. Inside their little shack, they closed their eyes and fell into a deep nap.

Irving soon began to awake from his tragic morning and third death. He coughed and choked his way around in the rocky harbor, splashing sea water high up into the air. When he finally opened his eyes, a ruthless wave came soaring over his head, threatening to kill him again right then and there. Irving puffed out his cheeks, held his breath and prayed for mercy.

Splash! The water barreled into him like a grenade, tossing his dapper, little body into unspeakable positions. "Help!" he cried from the small corner of his mouth poking out of the water. "Can't....swim!"

Life Four

In a second of relief from the oncoming waves, Irving spotted the dock and began to attempt to swim back, quickly realizing some sort of rope had twisted itself around his paws. After being suddenly yanked down into the cold waters, Irving felt his lungs balloon and nearly explode into a million pieces. Suddenly, he was thrown out of the water and high into the air. With his legs wriggling out of control, he slammed headfirst onto a crackling, wooden floor. Dozens of tiny fish savagely flapped their tails, gasping for their last breath. Their eyes bugged out from their slimy bodies as their lives slowly slipped away. Irving looked up from the destruction and found himself lying on a fishing boat deck. It wasn't Joe's, and it wasn't Jack's. Somebody else had caught him in his fishing net. Sooner or later he'd be fillet of cat.

Unaware of Irving's presence, the man on board began his fishly duties. He started by grabbing the plumpest fish. That's where the big money was. "Here's a fat one," the fisherman said with cigarette breath. He then reached for some sort of blade and scraped the fish bodies of their colorful scales until he achieved a certain grin of satisfaction. Irving hid under what he could, pulling the fish to his ears and around his paws just like he had done in the bucket. One of them lay dead with its mouth open wide enough for Irving to see all the way into its body. Wretched!

Irving lay shivering when George, the fisherman, finally found him. "Whadawe have here?" he laughed, yanking Irving by the tail. With his tattooed arm, he lifted Irving high above his head. "I think you're a cat!" he said as he stared into Irving's glossy eyes. "I ain't talking no catfish!" he laughed to himself out of utter amusement. "What should I do with you?"

Irving wriggled and writhed his body around, hoping to leap free and head back to the alley. It did no good at all. None whatsoever.

George slapped Irving onto the scaling table and grabbed his blade with one hand, holding Irving down with the other. Irving shivered all over and lamented about coming to this city at all. George drooled and foamed from his mouth with wicked pleasure. He jerked Irving's tail up high and with his other hand, brought the blade sailing down. He was going to skin him alive.

With all his might, Irving leapt from the table, swatted George across the face, knocking his blade right onto the floor.

"Youch!" George howled, grabbing his bloody forehead.

Irving jumped off the boat and swam like he never knew possible. Out of the water he charged, bolting down the dock and out of sight. Not once looking back, he left a lingering smell of fish in his path. As he got farther away, Irving's breath began to catch up with him. He stopped to rest on the sidewalk.

Irving stared down the street. No fisherman running behind. I got away, he sighed, water dripping from his ears. Deciding to lick the fishy bits from his fur, Irving looked down at his soaked body and made a horrible discovery. Blood! I'm bleeding! It was then he noticed the cut across his belly. His high-speed getaway had him so consumed with escaping, he hadn't even felt his fatal injury. It seems George got him after all. It would be ten minutes before enough blood drained out his fourth life. Irving lay dead, again.

As Romeo came down from his hallucinatory state, he told Candle the puzzling story. She was stunned but grateful Romeo had finally opened up to her for the first time in years. She hadn't decided if what he was saying could possibly be true, still she believed he thought it was. That was enough to convince her. "We must go to the Factory," Romeo explained, already heading back. "I've got to ask others to help me."

As Romeo and Candle made for home, a distant church bell rang. "Four o'clock!" Romeo cried. "We haven't got much time. The others will be heading for their homes soon!"

"But Romeo," Candle broke in, "how are you going to do that? Everyone is mad at you!"

Romeo looked back at her with wonder. "What do you mean, everyone's mad at me? What are you talking about?"

"Wise up, Romeo! You've been nothing but a pest for the last two years!" Candle exploded.

Chapter Seven

"How can you be so oblivious to what ill will you've created?"

"That's crazy. You're wrong!"

Candle kept quiet the rest of the way. Could Romeo be that naive? Candle carried her head low and only spoke when she needed to give a direction. "Turn right at the light. Go straight. Look out for the pothole."

Romeo carefully studied the buildings and street shops in hopes of memorizing them for next time. At his age, he felt he knew it all. He didn't like relying on someone else to get around, especially a female.

The neighborhoods were starting to look livelier the farther they traveled away from the schoolyard. People were out on the streets, and eager marathoners were squeezing in one last workout before the big day. Candle watched their feet splash by her and followed their shadows with her eyes. One in particular whirled by at an incredible speed. But it wasn't a human. It was a cat. "Did you see that Alley run by?" she asked Romeo, still feeling the trail of wind left by the zooming cat. "It was going awfully fast!"

Ignoring her, he pulsed forward. What Candle had seen was actually Calvin racing towards Buggles's hideout on a suspicious hunch.

When Calvin reached Buggles's place, he climbed up the building in the usual way. Being very careful, he crept as close as he could to the window and pressed his ear against a crack in the glass. He first heard a lot of nothing, just some talk of bread and onions and somebody named

Life Four

Grizelle. But he still had that sinking feeling. He listened on. As he suspected, the conversation started to get interesting.

"...are you really going to get away with that?" Chip asked. "What if somebody sees you?"

"Not to worry," Buggles's voice answered. "Besides, have I ever let you down?"

Calvin curled his tail under his belly and chewed it in his mouth. What could this mean? he wondered.

Calvin heard a long pause and knew the bomb was ready to fall. "The very first cat I see at that stupid marathon," Buggles continued in his smarmy sort of way, "I'm gonna steal and blow him up! Ha!"

"Whoa! I can't wait to see that!" Chip cheered.

Outside, Calvin listened to the horrifying news. He had to warn all the Sticks of this maddening development. But would anyone believe him? They had to. They simply had to. In a flash, he was back on the street racing toward the Factory.

Chapter Eight

Romeo and Candle were growing closer to the Factory by the minute. Above them, early signs of evening dribbled in as the flickering sun began its nightly decent into the five o'clock haze. Romeo had to hurry for he knew many of the Factory Sticks would soon be heading home to their families. Something he hadn't done in years.

"Hurry, Candle!" Romeo cried. "We've got to go faster!"

"I'm trying! I'm trying!" Candle blared.

As they got even closer to the Factory,

Life Four

Candle spotted something dreadful up ahead. "Oh, my!" she shouted. "Look! There's a dog!"

Romeo heard her through the wind and quickly adjusted his eyes with a tight squint. Candle was wrong. At the end of the next block was a stocky, gruesome looking rat with a long, sharp tail. Anger instantly soared through Romeo. It wasn't Hog, but it was definitely one of his clan. Without a moment to spare, Romeo made an instant decision.

"Keep going!" he shouted back at Candle as the rat became clearer, it's tiny red-hot pupils burning like two hot coals. "It's a rat! Don't stop!"

Those words registered in Candle's brain, though she didn't believe it. "That's a rat?" she cried, eying the tail as it zipped back and forth. The rat was standing on his hind legs against the high street curb, swinging its tail in large, arrogant circles. Its pointy nose was a bright orange.

"No ordinary rat!" Romeo added wondering why the rat was out on the streets to begin with. Didn't they have to stay underground?

Romeo ran faster and faster. He took one sideways glance at the rat as he rocketed by. The rat glared back. "Go!" Romeo screamed. Candle and Romeo flew by as swiftly as they could.

"We're gettin' hungry, my friend!" the rat called out in a cocky voice. "Can you hear my stomach growl? I hope you're getting everything… ready for us!"

"What'd he say?" Candle howled just as the

rat's tail slowly disappear into the filthy gutter.

"Come on, Candle!" Romeo shouted. "We're almost to the Factory." Candle kept quiet the rest of the way.

Bait and Cheeseburger finished their third spider of the day. For desert, they rummaged through a pile of old magazines. "I knew we should've never hired that crummy, no-good cat!" Bait snapped, thinking of Irving. "He's been gone for a really, really long time! Where's my fishies?" He flipped through a magazine eying the restaurant ads and recipe pictures.

"Yeah, he's nothin' but a loooser!" Cheeseburger giggled, teasing a plump roach with his hungry eyes. "I'm tired of these wiggly guys," he confessed. "I want some real food! Like dat one!" He pointed to a picture of pot roast. Cheeseburger looked down at his pudgy, chunky body. "I'm wasting away!"

"You's too fat!" Bait whined.

"Too fat, eh?" Cheeseburger growled. "You's too ugly!"

"Oh, yeah?"

"Yeah!"

This went on and on and on. Thankfully, that poor little roach escaped unharmed and happy.

Romeo charged through the Factory door at 5:30 P.M. His journey left him sweaty and exhausted but no less determined. He knew his only hope for succeeding in this mission was to get help from the Factory Sticks.

Life Four

Candle flew in next. She too was weary and weak and in need of immediate rest. Like Romeo, she ran down the long corridor and soon found herself in the buzzing rec room. Luckily because of tomorrow's grand reopening celebration, many Sticks were still around working out the final kinks before the festivities began. In the midst of their joy and excitement for the coming day, all stopped and stared as Romeo took center stage.

"Where's Mr. Sox? I've got to find Mr. Sox!" Romeo shouted.

"He's not here!" Fluffy cried back.

"Well, where is he?" Romeo snapped. Candle stood back with worry in her eyes.

"I said he's not here, Romeo!" Fluffy reiterated with a bitter sound to his voice.

From behind the couch, Mr. Shadow stood up tall and walked over to the young male. "Is there something I can help you with, Romeo?" he said as a large string broke free from his yellow sweater and dangled below his belly.

"Look, I need Mr. Sox," Romeo said again. "It's very important..."

"He's at a shrink!" Mr. Gamble yelled.

Romeo looked up to find his father glaring down at him. "What's a shrink?" he asked.

Mr. Gamble took a step closer. With his back paw, he reached an itch near his signature diamond marking. "A shrink is a doctor of the mind," he began, pointing to his head. "Mr. Sox needs advice on how to get through to you! In fact, all of us do!"

"Huh? What are you talking about?" Romeo cried. He turned to look for Candle. He knew she was on his side. He spotted her crouching alone in the darkness as some of the other Sticks began to walk away. This was becoming a father-son thing, and nobody wanted to get involved. "Where's everybody going?" Romeo asked. "I've got to tell you something."

"We don't want to hear about it, man," Twinkle Toes said from the comfort of his favorite cat bed, a large wok and a bag of stuffing. He often waited there at the end of the day for somebody who could walk him home safely. Ever since he found happiness with Gwen, he didn't take any chances. "You been tripping lately, and frankly, I'm sick of it, man," Toes admitted with no regret.

"Listen to me! If we don't do something quick, the rats are going to get Dennis!" Romeo cried with glossy eyes. "They're going to... they're going to...they're going to bust him up, or something worse! It's true!"

"Who would hurt Dennis? Who?" Mr. Shadow asked as he tugged the string off his yellow sweater.

"The rats!" Romeo yelled. "I already told you, the rats!" Romeo began to circle the room in a frenzy.

"Rats? Rats?" Snickers said with drool oozing from his mouth. "Where? I could go for a juicy rat right about now!"

Life Four

"No, you don't understand!" Romeo began. "You can't eat these rats! They're the big ones from Vent City! Remember?"

Fluffy knew those rats well. They nearly killed him that first day in the vents. "Is this some kind of joke, Romeo?" he asked with his tail wagging high in the air. "Because if it is, I'll be..."

"It's no joke!" Romeo insisted. "They said if I don't bring them all kinds of food tomorrow, they'll get Dennis! They're mad at me! Don't you believe me?"

"That's the most ridiculous thing I've ever heard!" Fluffy snapped.

"Son, son," Mr. Gamble said, "just sit down and tell us slowly. Now, do you mean Hog and his colony?"

"You know Hog?" Romeo asked surprised. "How?"

"I lived in Vent City, remember?"

Romeo took a moment to catch his quickening breath. "Yes, those rats! I have to get all the food at the marathon and put it in the taxi before seven o'clock, so you all have to help me or it'll never get done!"

"Taxi? What taxi?" MayBell asked with streamers still in her paw.

"Are you cats even listening to me? I said..."

"It's true!" Candle suddenly erupted. "It's all true!"

Mr. Gamble walked slowly up to Candle

who still hovered near the back of the room. "Do you know about this taxi, my dear?"

"Well, I didn't actually see it, but I believe..."

"And did you speak to the rats as well?"

"Not exactly," Candle mumbled, "but I know Romeo did. And I did see one..."

"This is nonsense! Nonsense!" Mr. Shadow piped in still pulling at that same string. It was growing into a big ball on the floor as the sweater grew shorter and shorter. "I think you're trying to sabotage tomorrow's party with this cockamamie story! Now tell us the truth, there are no rats and this whole thing is a lie! A Lie!" The string finally broke just before the sweater reached his neck. His two sleeves and collar were all that remained.

Romeo stood stunned at Shadow's accusations and all the frowning faces around him. "Why don't you believe me?" He looked to his father. "Dad?" Mr. Gamble shook his head and turned away.

"You don't care about us anymore! You haven't for a long time!" Fluffy shouted. "Why should we believe you now?"

Romeo stood back. "Is that what you think?" he snapped. "All right, maybe I haven't been the life of the party lately, but I've never lied! Never!" He headed for the front door. "If you're not going to help me, then fine! I'll do it myself! You'll see! I'll do it myself!"

In a flash Romeo was gone. Candle dashed

after him. Mr. Shadow and the others shook their heads and wondered.

A little while later, Calvin came bursting into the Factory in much the same way Romeo had earlier. Huffing and puffing, he flung himself on the couch with great theatrics in front of the same busy crowd of Sticks. He took advantage of any dramatic situation. It was the actor in him.

"Don't tell us, man," Twinkle Toes began with a giggle, "the rats are after you, right? They want grub or something?"

The few remaining Sticks laughed at the snide remark, although Calvin remained intensely serious. "Rats!" he cried. "No! Worse! Much worse!"

"Here we go again," Mr. Shadow mumbled feeling awfully silly in his shrunken sweater. "Tell us, Calvin," Shadow began, "what's going on?"

In great detail Calvin gave one of his finest performances yet. Using his own carefully rehearsed method, Calvin reenacted the conversation between Buggles and Chip. He played all the roles, even using props. The Sticks watched with dropped jaws. "I'll ruin da first one I see!" Calvin said trying to replicate Buggles's heavy accent and stern tone. "At the finish line!" he concluded with his paw raised in the air.

"Well, this is just terrible! Terrible!" Mr. Shadow cried, always double wording when he wanted to be extra serious.

"We've got to be on alert!" Mr. Gamble warned. "This lunatic just might be the end of one

Chapter Eight

of us! He's obviously snapped!" Gamble walked in circles holding his head down and mumbling ideas to himself. "Nobody can be alone between now and tomorrow! The opening ceremony must be postponed!" A heavy sigh spun through the room like a deflated balloon. Another disappointment.

"But Romeo?" Fluffy called. "What about Romeo?"

"What do you mean, Fluffy?" Mr. Shadow asked.

Fluffy pointed to the door. "He's out there!"

The room grew silent.

Outside in the cold, frigid air, Romeo paced up and down the streets desperately searching for that taxi. His nose was like ice, and his paws blistered from the long stretches of running. *I may as well run the marathon*, he thought. He'd probably win.

Romeo balanced dizzily on his paws, swaying back and forth with the wind. With no food in his belly and hardly a wink's sleep, he stumbled around as all the buildings and street signs grew blurry and distorted. They began to twist and bend like licorice whips. His body was going to give up. It was inevitable.

Just as he was about to collapse, something else happened. "What do we have here?" cried a suspicious male voice wrapped in a long, brown raincoat. "I think I spot a cat!"

"Are you gonna take him?" asked another

stranger. Romeo's ears perked up.

"You bet I am!" roared the first. "This is what I been waitin' for!"

From a safe distance, Candle watched helplessly as Romeo was savagely scooped up and taken away. Her eyes widened, and she threw her paw to her mouth in horror. That must be him! she thought, contemplating charging after them and clawing them to skinny shreds. But she couldn't take them on alone, and Romeo was too weak to help. That must be Buggles!

Candle rushed back to the Factory. She had to get help.

Deep in the city, Irving awoke with a pounding headache. In fact, something was pounding it. Oh, my! Irving cried as he came to. What is going on here?

"Do it again, Mitch!" twelve-year-old Doug called to his buddy. "Poke the kitty again!"

While Irving lay powerless on the concrete, two neighborhood bullies took great pleasure in knocking him around. Irving wanted nothing more than to leap up and scratch the dickens out of them, but having just lost another life, he was weak and defenseless and about to get the beating of his life, his fifth life to be exact.

"You got him good that time!" Doug cheered, seeing Mitch yank Irving's tail. It snapped back in a perfect curl.

Irving hissed and wiggled on the ground, but it was no use. The boys weren't finished.

Chapter Eight

As Doug was about to kick him yet again, they spotted an old lady walking by. They decided it was best to get away from any witnesses. After all, their parents had a lot of friends in this part of town who would be more than happy to flap their big mouths if they were seen. "We better get outta here," Mitch suggested, "before someone sees us.

"We could go to my place!" Doug said. "Mom and Pop's ain't there! We'll have the whole place to ourselves!"

"Lead the way!" Mitch agreed. With Irving clenched tightly under his arm, Mitch carried him the full three blocks. Irving meowed to a passing baby in a stroller, hoping for some sort of assistance. Didn't work.

Before he knew it, the boys were huffing up a short, concrete staircase, the kind with cracks and holes. This is bloody awful! Irving thought to himself.

Doug opened the door to his musty apartment. An immediate whiff of sour milk came whirling into the green painted hallway. Doug took one peek inside to make sure the coast was clear. When positive his parents weren't home, he tossed Irving inside much like he did his father's morning newspaper. Irving tumbled onto the frayed couch like a rag doll. His fur was still smelly from the fish, but Mitch and Doug didn't care. They had their owns smells to worry about.

"Let's take him out back!" Mitch roared, heading for the back door. Doug's building had a backyard that all the tenants shared. It was so neglected hardly anyone ever went back there. "Come on! Let's go!"

Outside the boys dragged Irving down the two back steps and into the patchy weed covered lawn. It was dark already as he was tossed into a thick puddle of mud in the middle of the yard. Squish! Mitch and Doug ran circles around him waving their arms and cackling like roosters. Irving sat up and rubbed the mud from his eyes.

"Let's put him in the tree!" Mitch cried. "You know, like in cartoons!"

"Cool!" Doug agreed.

It was right about that time Irving finally began to get some strength back. Sure, he had been knocked around pretty badly, but he still had some fight left. *I've got to get myself out of his horrid place!* he cried to himself.

But before Irving could do anything, he was being tossed up into a tall tree. From the high branch, he looked down at his two amused attackers as they fell into hysterics. "Look at him shake!" Mitch cried.

"He'll never get down! Never!" Doug added.

They were right. Irving would be up there for a long time.

When Romeo got over his initial shock, he found himself in Buggles's apartment. Romeo didn't know it, but because of being

133

in the wrong place at the wrong time, he had just become Buggles's prime target.

Romeo was held in a deep cardboard box. The top was closed, and the only thing piercing through the darkness was the light from two tiny puncture holes in the side. Romeo was beside himself with worry. He had to get back out there on the streets. *This sucks!* he cried to himself. *Now how am I going to get that darn food?*

Mr. Sox walked into the Factory just as Fluffy and Mr. Shadow were leaving. He noticed right away the familiar look of panic on their faces as they walked past him down the hall. "Is there something wrong, gentlemen?" Mr. Sox asked stopping in front of a cereal box painting of Lulu, the Factory's creator.

Fluffy let his head fall and waited for Mr. Shadow to speak. "Huff," Mr. Shadow let out a heavy sigh and began. "Calvin came to warn us of Buggles Flannigan."

"Who's Buggles Flannigan?" asked Mr. Sox. "I've never heard that name mentioned before."

"Sure you have. Buggles was Calvin's catnapper, remember?" Mr. Shadow said.

"Oh, yes. Now I remember," Mr. Sox said quickly. "What's wrong? Is there something the matter?"

"Mr. Sox, why don't you come back inside with me." Mr. Shadow led Mr. Sox back into the Factory allowing Fluffy to continue on home to his family with some other Sticks.

Life Four

Chapter Eight

In the rec room, Shadow explained the puzzling situation to Mr. Sox. "What do you think, Mr. Sox?" Shadow concluded, spraying Sox's wire rimmed glasses with a gentle mist of spit.

"This is terrible!" exclaimed Mr. Sox, taking off his glasses and wiping them on a pillow. "I quite agree with Gamble. This is a pickle!" he said having heard Mr. Gamble's suggestions. "The ceremony must be postponed until further notice. At least until the Buggles situation has had time to cool off." With one, swift move, he put his glasses back on his head and rubbed his nose clean. "The poor Sticks, they've been so looking forward to tomorrow. I hate to tell them the bad news."

"What exactly should we do?" Mr. Shadow asked.

"It's best to keep everybody inside and out of harm's way. For those already at their homes, we must warn them before they venture out tomorrow."

"But how will we do that Mr. Sox? If we have to stay inside who will go warn them about Buggles?"

Mr. Sox hadn't thought of that. No doubt, being the smart cookie that he was, he should have. After a moment, Mr. Sox had an idea. "Shadow," he said. "We haven't used the City Chime in years. In fact, I don't even know if it still works. It's time to give it a try."

Life Four

"The City Chime!" Mr. Shadow cried. "I thought that was a thing of the past! An old ghost! Kaput!"

Mr. Sox stared oddly at the tip of Shadow's nose. A tiny speck of bright, blue paint slept between his nostrils. "Not in your lifetimes has it been used, Shadow," Mr. Sox said as he paced in front of him. "True, it's rusty and ancient, but it's worth a try!"

The City Chime was a device created by the first Sticks during the torturous reign of Carnival. It was implemented as a means of warning the Sticks when a potential Alley invasion was under way. Although intended as a marvel of engineering, its low success rate banished it from being used, but like Sox said, it was worth one more go.

With its loud horn and genius construction, the chime had a reverb of several miles in each direction, just enough to reach every nook and cranny of the city. Its use had been discussed on previous occasions, such as the early threats with Fidel and the Vent City revolt, but it was feared that if sounded, the bell would defeat the Sticks's purpose, for Fidel had known of its existence. However, Fidel had supposedly been the only recent Alley who had any knowledge of it. It was constructed long before Bait, Max, or any of the other Alleys. Fidel knew of its legend through the stories passed down from his ancestors, the Alley leaders. With them and Fidel dead, it would now be the perfect solution for the Sticks. The warning bell would ring, and everyone would know what to do. One ring meant head to the Factory, two rings, stay at home.

Just then, Mr. Gamble came soaring down in the newly remodeled soup pot elevator. A temporary model. Nobody was able to locate an actual soup pot after the other had been destroyed by the Alleys, so an old bedpan had temporarily been installed. The job of locating it had been given to Uncle Fred as a sympathy project to lift his spirits after being ridiculed for a series of bad decisions. After two months, the bedpan was all he could find. He spotted the dented thing lying in a garbage dump alongside some old hubcaps and torn-up playing cards. Because of all the rain, Uncle Fred figured it was clean enough, especially after he gave it a once over with his tongue. Even he had to hold his nose for that one. Together, he and two other Sticks carefully lugged it to the Factory only scratching the rim and making a minimal disturbance. Only one bum saw them, but he was preoccupied eating a hard slice of beef jerky with no teeth. He watched the cats and their "port-a-potty" from his bloodshot eyes.

And so, the bedpan became the latest feature of the newly refurbished Factory. It promised to be a big hit at the party. Darla had decorated it with ribbons and a touch of that pretty blue paint. Though functional, it was still a bedpan. Of course, in the future everyone had high hopes of finding another real soup pot like their old faithful.

Life Four

"Mr. Shadow! Mr. Sox! You're back!" Mr. Gamble yelled, climbing his way out of the elevator. "Did you hear the news? Did you hear about Romeo?"

"Romeo?" Mr. Sox asked, looking at Mr. Shadow. "What does this have to do with Romeo?"

Embarrassment shone all over Mr. Shadow's face, for that was one important detail he had forgotten to mention. "Romeo ran out into the street," Shadow admitted, itching his neck under his sweater. "He's running around in the city all alone! He...he doesn't know about Buggles!"

"Well, this is just terrible!" Mr. Sox shouted. "I say we ring that chime immediately! There might be others out there too!" Mr. Sox walked deeper into the room and right up to Mr. Gamble. "Gamble," he began, "he's your son. What do you think we should do?"

Mr. Gamble paused and stared blankly at Mr. Sox. He couldn't remember a time when Sox asked for his opinion on such an important matter. But Sox was getting older. He'd been a niner for longer than anyone could remember. In fact, it was a miracle to everyone he'd lasted this long. Aside from his inevitable future, he was pushing eighty in people years. While he still had his mind and infinite wisdom, his body and his strength were giving out. As of late, he often dealt out the more rigorous Factory jobs and tasks he would have once taken upon himself to other younger, more agile Sticks.

Chapter Eight

Mr. Gamble thought about the question, then finally answered, thinking only of Romeo. "I'm going to find him myself. I lost him once. I'm not losing him again!"

"But what about ringing the City Chime?" Mr. Sox asked. "Do you understand how it works? Don't you think it's worth a try before you travel out alone? You could get catnapped, and what good would that do?"

Mr. Gamble bathed in flattery at another of Sox's questions. He had read of the Chime in the Stick library one afternoon when he was restacking some old books. "Yes, it's worth a try, but a father must do what a father must do. I have to go out there. I might not find Romeo, but at least maybe he'll hear the warning and be alerted."

"I understand," Sox agreed. He then turned to Mr. Shadow and squinted. "Now Shadow, just one concern."

"What's wrong, Mr. Sox?"

"I'm trying to think back to Combat School. Shadow, was there mention of the bell to the students?" Sox said slowly "They do know of its existence, don't they?" He looked at Mr. Shadow with questioning eyes and heavy suspicion.

Shadow's blood sunk to his paws. He hadn't considered that until this very moment. "Uh...of course! Of course...they know about...the bell!" As he talked, his voice twitched and a silly, nervous smirk appeared on his greasy face. "We went over it a hundred times! Two hundred times!

They know what to do when they hear that bell!"
Mr. Sox increased his fearful look of intensity as
Mr. Shadow struggled on. "Sure they do! Sure!"

Mr. Gamble peered at him. In his years at
the Factory, he had heard and seen for himself
evidence of Mr. Shadow's sloppy work ethic and
his often, though unintentional, careless behavior.
"You don't sound very...positive," Mr. Gamble
sneered. "If you're not telling the truth, it could
mean Romeo's life and the others too!"

Mr. Shadow dusted himself off and knocked
a lone bead of sweat from his head. "Well, I think
we talked about the bell. I know it was in my lesson
plan," he said quickly, inching back farther and
farther. "I'd have to ask Waffles and Vittles. They
were teachers too, remember?" he concluded with
a phony smile and a shrug. "Maybe they talked
about the bell."

"They wouldn't have!" Mr. Sox sniped. "It
would have been in your class! Doesn't sound
to me like the Sticks know anything about the
City Chime! They'll just think it's a church bell!
Shadow, this is a disgrace!"

Mr. Shadow curled into a tiny ball and hid
under what remained of his sweater. His shoulders
dropped with the weight of all the shame he felt.
How could he have not talked about the warning
bell? How could he have missed such a simple
solution to so many problems in the city? Sure, it
hadn't been used in years, but that was no excuse.
He had a duty to the Sticks, and he failed. It was

time to pay. Everyone's lives were in his paws. Shadow had never known such a sickening feeling of guilt. He barfed twice.

Mr. Sox took in a deep breath and continued. "There's only one thing to do, gentlemen," he began calmly. "Mr. Shadow, you are going to have to join Mr. Gamble out there. Find Romeo and warn any others."

"Maybe we should go back and get Fluffy," Mr. Shadow suggested. "He could help us look. Besides..."

"No! He's better off at home!" Mr. Sox snapped, pacing in tiny circles. "I don't understand what's going on around here, Shadow!" he roared. "You're the one who didn't teach anyone about the warning bell! You're the one who's going to go find Romeo!"

Mr. Shadow felt microscopic. Not a good feeling. "Maybe we're overreacting," he said as a sudden thought sprang to mind. "We're getting all worked up over something Calvin said! Think about it! Calvin!"

"So, what's your point?" Mr. Gamble asked.

"He's an actor! He exaggerates! He probably made it all up!"

Mr. Sox walked up very close to Shadow. "Can you think of one single time when he has ever lied to you about anything?"

"Well, no. I guess not, but..."

"There you have it!" Mr. Sox exploded. He

sat down. "Mr. Shadow," he continued, calming himself. "I have always respected you, but if you are going to fight me, then maybe I've been wrong about you all this time. We've had a legitimate warning from an upstanding stick! Now if you don't act immediately, then you are no longer welcome here!"

Mr. Gamble's jaw dropped.

"Please, no, Mr. Sox!" Shadow whined. "I'll go! I'll go right now!" With his head still buried, he wobbled over to the front door knocking into everything. "See? I'm going! You'll see! I'll find Romeo! I will! Will!"

Mr. Sox watched Shadow's pathetic exit. He turned to Gamble and said, "Gamble, go with him. Find your son."

Mr. Gamble hurried out the door.

Octavian had been watching from the corner of the room. When the entertainment finally ended, he returned to a meeting in progress. His team of spiders was busy designing the arachni-coaster for their upcoming park. It promised to be a huge hit.

Chapter Nine

Irving had been left for dead after being used as a feline punching bag.

He pleaded with his tormentors as he shrieked at the top of his lungs, but they got him! They got him good! By the time their little game was over, Irving had two swollen eyes, a bleeding bald spot, and one broken eardrum. He was a mess, to say the least.

"I thinks he's a goner!" Irving heard just before he fell into a near-death spiritual place. The all-too-familiar tingling sensation he felt four times before had caught up with him once again. His tortured soul soared down the usual path, swirling endlessly in the same old dark and echoed tunnel. Blah, blah, blah. He was dead... again. After more of the usual afterlife mumbo-jumbo, Irving began to awake into life six.

RAP! RAP! RAP! One of the boys tapped on him. When Irving started to move, the boys took immediate notice and jumped back.

"Whoa! What's the deal? That dude was dead, wasn't he?" Mitch checked Irving's tail and peeked into his eyes.

Doug circled the tree with a mysterious look. He rubbed his chin that would one day grow the beard he always dreamed of with his marker stained hands and thought harder and longer than he ever had before. "Guess not!" he said after about nine empty seconds. Nothing too smart ever came out of him. Nothing.

"Should we throw him down the garbage shoot?" Mitch said devilishly, poking Irving in the belly. "Or how's about flushin' him down the can? It worked on my sister's mouse!"

"Naw, I've got a better idea. Come on! Follow me!"

With his eyes swelled shut, Irving could feel himself being dragged once again inside. He was tossed onto the floor while the two boys left the room. ...got to get out..., Irving said robotically. ...must leave now. But by the time Irving finally managed to lift just one paw, the boys had returned after making quite a racket. They snatched him up by the neck and began their next cruel adventure.

Chapter Nine

"This is gonna be fun!" Doug roared.

With a tight, sharp rope, Irving was strapped down to some sort of small, metal box with all sorts of cold knobs and things. He couldn't move, he couldn't see, and he couldn't escape.

"Let her rip!" Doug howled. Irving heard a loud click, and all of a sudden, he was off! Soaring forward!

"Yee-haw!" the boys yelled. Irving cracked open one puffy eye and saw...

An electric train! They strapped me to an electric train!

With the controls in his hand, the maniacal train conductor slammed Irving into the wall, then back again. The boys drooled like dogs, enjoyment beaming from every pour, goose bumps inching up their lanky arms. "Ha! Ha! Ha!" they cheered.

"Do it again!"

Irving continued to wiggle and hiss, his head slapping back and forth against the wall.

"Back him up as far as he can go, then let him have it!" Doug cried.

Slowly and carefully, Conductor Mitch steered the train all the way to the far end of the long tracks. Irving saw the wall looming in front of him like a battlefield.

"Wow! Watch him go!"

Like a rocket, Irving and the train flew and flew until...BANG! It was all over.

"Whoo-hoo!" the boys hollered.

Like a limp doll, Irving hung over the toy

train, a little piece of fish still in his ear.

Suddenly, Doug spotted his parents coming up the sidewalk. They were good, solid people. A far cry from Doug. "What are they doing back?" he shrilled. "They ain't supposed to be here!"

The boys could hear the doorknob starting to turn. "Quick! Throw him outside!" Doug yelled.

With that, Irving was tossed out the back door. "We'll go back for him later," Mitch cried.

Like two little angels, the boys quickly grabbed some books and flung themselves on the couch. "Hello, fellas," Doug's mom said as they walked into the room. "Doing homework? That's nice. I'll make you boys some cookies." She walked into the kitchen to fix a snack as the boys hi-fived with evil glee.

On her way back to the Factory, Candle decided to search for a taxi she wasn't even sure existed. Based on Romeo's description, his cab could have been any one of dozens. In the darkness, Candle swirled through intersections and mazes of the city finding nothing. Her situation was getting hopeless.

After a while, she stopped to rest. Her paws were aching, and her fur was cold. Under a gray and warm awning, she stretched her legs and sat beside a large, wooden Indian. It seemed to look down at her as if it were angry. Candle decided to give up on her search and return to the Factory. She wasn't far away.

"Did you find him?" Mr. Sox asked with an

urgency in his voice, looking behind her. "Do you have Romeo?"

Candle stood in front of him wide eyed and panting. Mr. Sox dropped his head low to the ground. He knew she didn't. "But what about Shadow and Gamble? Did you see them? Did they find anything?"

"Mr. Sox I...," Candle began hesitantly, tears welling up in her eyes. "I've got something to tell you..."

"What is it, my child?" Mr. Sox asked. "I'm listening."

Candle inched closer, her watery eyes drifting around the room. "I don't know how to say this," she began with a lump in her throat, "but I saw two men steal Romeo! They took him away!" She burst into tears.

"Are you sure? Absolutely sure? Two men? Romeo?"

Candle nodded her head and collapsed into Mr. Sox's paws. "I was going to attack them, but I just froze!" She sniffled and whined as Mr. Sox bit his bottom lip in anger.

"Those scoundrels," he mumbled. "They got our boy! They got our boy!"

Romeo huddled deep in his cardboard chamber. "Here's how it's gonna work," Buggles explained to Chip over a sloppy drawing of the marathon route. "You'll stand here, and I'll come in with the cat over here." He turned and twisted the crinkled map in several directions inspecting every last corner of the race route.

"I don't understand," Chip said blankly.

Buggles rolled his eyes and flattened the map with his hand. "All right, look again, Chip. Right here is you," he pointed, "and here is where I'll stand. Got it?"

"Huh? Where do I go?"

A crimson red began to blush across Buggles's face. "Here is where you stand! Okay?"

"No. Can you go over it one more time?"

By now, Buggles's lips were pinched so tightly, they had curled completely around his teeth. "Get outta here! I don't wanna look at your face anymore!"

"Man, ask a simple question," Chip said as he swaggered down the hall. "Boy, oh boy...," he mumbled into his bedroom.

And with that, Buggles stormed out the front door dragging his long coat behind him. As soon as Romeo heard the door slam shut, he let out a massive sigh of relief. But he wasn't in the clear yet. Hardly. He had a long way to go.

By about nine o'clock in the bitter evening, Mr. Gamble and Mr. Shadow met back at the Factory. Fluffy had returned as well. They knew there was only one thing left to do.

"We've got to go to Buggles's apartment," Mr. Gamble decided. "Surely Romeo's there." He was convinced of that after hearing Candle's account of what she saw. "The catnapper has struck again."

Chapter Nine

"But where does he live?" Fluffy asked smartly. "Calvin's the only one who knows."

Mr. Sox carefully removed his spectacles and rubbed his tired eyes. After a moment, he put them back on his nose, stood up straight and tall, and gave his orders. "Shadow, ring the City Chime," he began with a wave. "It may not work, but it's worth a try." Shadow nodded and headed up to the tower. "Gamble, stay here with me, and we'll come up with an escape plan. Fluffy and Candle, go to Calvin's apartment. No doubt he's home with Lloyd. Make Cal lead you to Buggles's hideout. Don't let him talk you out of it!" Sox stood back and took in a deep drag off his pipe. "You're all to meet at the Factory at ten o'clock sharp," he added eying everyone in the room. "Go at once!"

In a flash, Fluffy and Candle flew outside and into the night. Fluffy knew the quickest way to Lloyd's apartment. "Follow me!" he yelled to Candle.

As they charged down the street, the late night city crawlers were coming out in droves. The human underground party scene was just getting started. Young teenage boys and girls dressed in long black clothes and gothic paraphernalia began migrating down the streets and into the after hours clubs. It was Saturday night, and a special holiday at that. Cryptor's Eve was the one night of the year the moon shone its brightest. It had been rumored that it was on this very night lost souls roamed the streets searching for their final

Life Four

resting place. It had become an annual festival for the late night dwellers. An evening like no other.

"So this is Cryptor's Eve," Candle said, hovering in the darkest spots on the sidewalk far away from the freaky teenagers. "I heard people talking about it today. Sure seems silly to me."

"Forget about it," Fluffy said, zigzagging between two made up vampires. "Just follow me and don't trail behind."

Candle took a good solid stare at the kids coming her way. They looked scary and mysterious. "I'm sticking to you like glue," she said, sliding up to him.

After a few more blocks, they arrived at Calvin's building. They stood on the sidewalk in the intense moonlight and stared up the ladder of windows. "Let's go," Fluffy said holding out his paw. Together they began to climb.

Sure enough, Calvin was snuggled up tightly to Lloyd's ankle. It was almost ten o'clock and the Sticks had no time to lose. They knew Mr. Sox wouldn't put up with any tardiness. Uncle Fred was the last to suffer the punishment of being late. A while back, he was tardy for some guard training. Mr. Sox made him dust all the library books with his tail. It took him the whole night.

"Whadawe do now?" Candle asked, poking her nose under the window pane. "I've never had to catnap anybody before."

Fluffy studied the situation, then said, "Don't worry, Candle. I'll handle this."

Life Four

A little while later, Fluffy and Candle marched through the Factory's doors right on schedule. Calvin, only half awake, dragged sluggishly behind. Gamble and Shadow had been waiting anxiously despite their pessimism. Mr. Shadow had tremendous guilt over the whole chime fiasco. Still, he climbed up the Factory's old smoke stack, through the years of soot, and rang it like it hadn't been rung before. He knew nobody heard it. They wouldn't know what it was even if they had. How could he have forgotten to teach about the chime? It was in his lesson plans. Teachers are always forgetting things.

Mr. Shadow paced back and forth, back and forth, wearing a long groove in the floor. "Oh, sit down already!" Mr. Gamble snapped with every ounce of anxiety in his body. "You're making me dizzy!"

Mr. Shadow gave Gamble a long and painful stare. Mr. Sox caught his eye. "Stop," he mouthed in his direction.

"I'm sure glad you dragged me out of bed for this," Calvin growled, sleep still in the crevices of his pasty eyes. "I was in the middle of the most magnificent dream. I was starring in..."

"You have to take us to Buggles!" Fluffy interrupted.

"He's got Romeo!" Candle exploded.

Calvin shook his groggy head. "What?" he rattled. "What do you mean? That's impossible!" Calvin closed his eyes and began to doze off again.

Chapter Nine

"You dummy, wake up!" Fluffy wailed.

Mr. Sox barged in on their conversation with an uncontrollable urge to yell. "Oh, knock it off already! Let's get to business! It's going to be a long night, and sooner or later your people will be missing you. We have to figure this out quickly and efficiently and with no arguing!"

"Sorry," Fluffy and Calvin whispered with lowered heads.

"You're right, Mr. Sox," Gamble said. "It's going to be a very long night thanks to those cat snatching thieves!"

"No sense getting excited," Shadow said. "We need you to remain calm and level headed."

"Calm? Level headed?" Mr. Gamble growled into Shadow's vacant eyes. "Let's see how calm you are the day someone steals your son and..."

"Now, now," Mr. Sox interrupted, slipping in between the two. "...this is exactly what I'm talking about. You must try to hold back your anger. Remember, we cats have enough anger to blame a lot of things on these days. Hold your head high. Don't let the anger take you too!"

Mr. Gamble took a conservative step back. "I'm sorry," he said without much emotion. "I don't know what's come over me. I just feel so overwhelmed. I guess I just miss Romeo. The old Romeo." He walked to the other side of the room and sat alone with his face in his paws.

Life Four

By eleven o'clock the small but steady group, along with Mr. Shadow, made it all the way to Buggles's shabby apartment building. Calvin took the lead. Many of them had never been on that block before, let alone stepped paws in the incredulous, foul aura that devoured Buggles's building.

"It's the smell of trouble," Candle said as she stared up the mighty wall. "As an Alley you learn to live with it."

"I keep forgetting you're an Alley," Fluffy remarked.

"That's the nicest thing you ever said to me," Candle replied with a smile.

Fluffy blushed and his whiskers curled.

After another long climb up the vines, the three Stick spies reached the infamous hideout while Mr. Shadow kept watch below.

"This is it," Calvin said with a shiver. "This is the place."

"Not exactly paradise, is it?" Candle teased as a crumpled beer can sailed out of a high window.

"Not exactly," Calvin mumbled watching it fall.

"Whadawe do now?" Candle asked, same as before.

Fluffy had another of his ideas. "Look, we can handle this," he began. "Lord knows we've had enough practice." Fluffy rubbed the sticky glass window with his paw, erasing a large smudge. "What a mess," he remarked, peering into the filthy apartment. "There's garbage and junk everywhere! Moldy cereal bowls! Broken bottles! Tons of dirty sox! He's worse than the dogs!" Fluffy had heard a story from Snickers about a time he accidentally stumbled into the dogs's central meeting house. It was a smelly, deep and gooey disaster. Snickers had nightmares for weeks.

"Do you see Romeo?" Candle asked. She gripped her chest with her right paw and drew her eyes together.

Fluffy glued his face to the glass. "No, no I don't," he said, looking harder. "But it's so messy, he could be anywhere!"

Calvin pushed his way up to the window. "Lemme see," he said with a shake in his voice. A resurgence of traumatic memories was not his idea of a good time, but it was the only way to know for sure. "I could probably tell you where he is. I know Buggles's mind."

Candle and Fluffy leaned back allowing Calvin to huddle up closer. His tail began to flop up and down, his shoulders were quivering, and they heard him gag. "I don't see anything unusual," he said, pulling away quickly. This was harder than he thought.

"Wait," Fluffy said, holding out his paw. "You barely even looked. Give it another try, please."

Calvin rolled his eyes and stepped forward. "I don't know why you're even bothering," he said nervously. "Romeo's nothing but trouble. Did I tell you that last week I heard him say...." Suddenly, Calvin stopped. His neck grew tense. Silence.

"What? What is it?" Fluffy said.

"Do you see him?" Candle whined. "Please tell me he's all right!"

Calvin rubbed the glass some more, clearing away his breath marks. "I think I saw something move."

"What do you mean?" Fluffy asked with quickening breath.

Calvin squinted his eyes. "I don't know, but...I think I saw that big box moving. Whoa!" he blared. "There it goes again!"

"Let me see!" Fluffy roared, bolting in front of him. "It moved! You're right! Calvin, you're right!"

"Is it Romeo?" Candle asked.

"I think so," Fluffy said, inspecting the tightly shut window. "If we could just open this a little bit," he continued with a struggle, "I think we could get in there and..."

"Get in there?" Calvin cried. "I ain't going in there! Not again! Not on your lives!" He cowered back into a tiny ball and began to suck his paw ferociously. The leaves bounced, and the branch almost gave way.

"Come on, Calvin," Fluffy said. "You know we gotta do this."

Calvin knew he was right, but he still continued to rattle and shake. Candle sat beside him and patted his sweaty head. "You and I will grab Romeo fast and get out," she said with a nod to Fluffy. "Nobody wants to be here any longer than they need to. Right?"

"Yeah," Fluffy said. "Don't worry, Cal. We'll be outta here soon."

After some careful thinking, Fluffy began to pry open the window with an old rusted knife he found back on the sidewalk. Its metal glare beamed up at him just at the right moment. Candle was in charge of retrieving it. She insisted.

"I've almost got it," Fluffy struggled as he jiggled the knife under the window. "Just a little more....there!" he sighed, sweat streaking down his face.

"Now what?" Candle asked. "We can't just waltz in there!"

Within seconds, Fluffy had squeezed his way under the wooden frame and into the hideout. The others watched nervously from the window. Fluffy slithered through and around the piles of rubbish...a broken television set, seventeen cigarette butts, and a host of other repugnant delights, finally reaching the box in question. He leapt on top of it. Although he loved playing in boxes, he knew he had to stay serious.

As his nails planted deeply into the cardboard, the box began to shake. Something was banging and clanging around in there like a caged beast.

"Romeo? Romeo, are you in there?" Fluffy whispered. "It's me! Fluffy!"

Silence. The box stood still. And then..."What

in the heck's going on in there?" Chip yelled from the toilet. "Bugs? You back?"

"Get outta there, Fluffy!" Calvin warned from the window. "Come on!"

Fluffy began to scramble around on the box. Inside, Romeo waited. "Who's der?" called Chip, bursting into the room holding a long mop that had never been used. Not even once. Chip's ugly, second hand trousers still hung loosely around his ankles. His bright, orange boxers nearly blinded Fluffy, but not enough to keep him around.

"Get outta here, you miserable creature!" Chip wailed as Fluffy leapt off the box. "Out I say! Out!"

Fluffy zoomed away just as Chip sent his mop sailing down with a loud WHACK! The box sunk in.

Fluffy let out a long hiss and zigzagged around the room, splashing through muck as he ran from Chip's evil wrath.

Candle had the window open as wide as possible. She stood back on the branch hurriedly waving Fluffy over. Shadow watched frightened from below.

Fluffy zoomed out the window and sailed all the way down the building taking Calvin and Candle with him. Chip ran in circles holding his broom high above his head. On the street below everyone quickly reunited with Mr. Shadow. They lay on the sidewalk dripping in disappointment. Above, Chip's smarmy little head stuck out the

Chapter Nine

window for one final look before he slammed it shut, pleased with himself. Inside the box, Romeo shivered. He had escaped the smash of the broom by a hair. Hopeful, he tried to hold onto the belief that his old friends would come back to rescue him.

Chapter Ten

Everyone had seen enough. They knew Romeo was in that dented box. They could smell him. As the night grew older, Candle and Shadow headed back to the Factory while Calvin and Fluffy swaggered home. Their people would be waking soon. Shadow's would just have to worry.

Candle pounded down the street thinking only of Romeo. Locked in a box, she said to herself. Doesn't get much worse than that. All around her, young costumed hooligans out for a fun Cryptor's Eve danced up and down the streets, smelling like the bums in City Park. They belted out vulgar

Chapter Ten

songs banned by the radio stations.

She crossed the street and heard some garbled, alarming noises, then smelled a most ungodly scent. "Dogs!" she exploded, recognizing that foul, sweaty stench. Deciding it best not to hang around, she bolted out of there quicker than she could say Bull. Good thing, too. She would have been horrified had she seen the poor defenseless cat presently being harassed by the dogs.

"What kinda name is Irving?" Bull teased between the brick alley walls.

"Let me go! Please let me go!" Irving begged.

But Bull just stood there, growling through his nasty, jagged teeth. His other cronies inched closer and closer as huge drops of drool bombed the alley floor.

Irving lay helplessly in the corner.

Bull stood over him and called out to his gang. "Let's get'm, boys!" he snarled.

Thus was the grisly end of life number six for unlucky Irving who had the misfortune of always being in the wrong place at the wrong time. Only three more lives to go.

Mr. Sox decided Shadow should return to Buggles's apartment for a late night stake out. He was chosen because of his knowledge of city safety, his passion for taking the lead, and frankly, no one else wanted to do it. Sox dealt out the strict instructions. Act fast and get immediate help if anything unusual should arise.

Life Four

As Fluffy and Calvin walked home together, Calvin was growing increasingly tired. His heavy eyelids drew together like magnets, his head dragging like the lower end of a teeter-totter. He longed to return to his reoccurring dream where he was bathing in a tub of tuna on top of the world's finest cat tree, secret compartments and all.

"Get a move on," Fluffy barked, checking out the partygoers. "I don't trust these kids. Once they get going, there's no telling what they'll do to Sticks like us. The last thing we need is a group of humans playing dirty tricks."

"Okay," Calvin grumbled, the sleep already forming in the cracks around his eyes as he imagined his bottom sinking into the creamy mayonnaise. "Whatever you say," he ended with an enormous yawn.

Fluffy could see Calvin was drifting, so he nudged him in the rear and yanked his tail.

"What's the big idea?" Calvin grumbled. "I'm awake! Just leave me alone!"

"I just want to make sure...," Fluffy began until something else caught his attention. Something scary.

"What's the matter?" Calvin whined, sensing danger. "Why'd you stop?"

Up the street and under a traffic light stood a villainous Alley. An Alley so synonymous with the word evil, it almost scared the fur off poor Calvin. It sat there in the extreme moonlight, eyes beaming at them like red lasers. Calvin slid over

Chapter Ten

to the wall in fright. Fluffy didn't dare move. He knew right away who it was. Bait. They hadn't seen him in a long, long time.

Bait spotted them, too. He stood at the end of the street like a school bully, his hulking shadow edging out for blocks. "Well, well, well," he began as he sucked out something foreign from between his brown teeth. "Whadawe have here? A couple of Sticks, eh?" he snarled with a burp.

Fluffy's eyes burned like fire. Painful memories of Bait swelled in his head, but he wouldn't let it break him down. He stood proud like a soldier, fearless and mean. Courageous. Determined. At least, that's how he appeared. His insides were a jumbled mess.

"You'd better watch it!" Bait growled with a hiss. "My partner's gonna get you just as soon as he gets back here, see?"

Fluffy rolled his eyes. "You guys don't scare us!" he exploded. "Especially that lazy, no good partner of yours! What's his name? Hotdog? Weinerschnitel?"

"It's Cheeseburger!" Bait snapped back.

"Whatever!" Fluffy wailed.

Just then, a pack of partygoers turned the corner right in front of Bait completely ruining his big moment. The kids paraded by in a massive wall of chains and black clothing. Fluffy shifted his body back and forth to keep Bait in view, but it was no use. By the time the kids passed, he was long gone.

Life Four

"Where'd he go? Where'd he go?" Fluffy asked staring down the long, empty street.

Calvin unstuck his scared self from the bricks and joined Fluffy near the curb. "What was he talking about?" he asked. "Who's Cheeseburger?"

"Cheeseburger, remember?" Fluffy teased, still staring down the street in disbelief. "You know, it's that guy Cheeseburger. That big, clumsy guy that's always hanging around him." Fluffy took one more look down the street. "Don't worry. He's harmless. We've got nothing to worry about."

"Then why do you look so worried, huh?"

"I don't know," Fluffy sighed. "Awe, it's nothing. Come on. Let's get home."

As they walked on, Bait stuck his head out from the dark shadows of the alley and smirked. But not for long. The Pound's rickety gray van lurked in the shadows inching up the street. A surprise visit.

Late in the evening, long after Candle and the others had given in to sleep, Irving stumbled into the street, his fur messy and wet. He began to bumble his way back to his cozy corner in Bait's Alley. The dogs had finally left, but he couldn't shake the fear from his body. He walked the city feeling disoriented and frail. In fact, he became so distracted, he smacked right into a telephone pole knocking himself out cold. He lay there unconscious under the glow of the moonlight.

As the city slept, the die-hard partiers had

their last go around before taking one final, blurry stare at the majestic moon. It wouldn't shine like that again until next year. Trails of the big night littered the streets. Cans, bottles, cigarette butts. Nothing kids this young should even know about. But in the big city, anything can happen and usually does.

Meanwhile, the skeleton crew of workers set up orange cones and banners for the early morning marathon. *First Annual City Run-a-Thon*, it said in bright, blue letters. *Presented by Salty Cat Food and Mr. Quivers's Traveling Side Show*. Many of the city employees had worked a pain-staking double shift to get the job done. After their long day of mending potholes or servicing phone lines, some were recruited for the marathon set-up crew. And it wasn't a time to turn down work. It never was.

By six A.M., much of the marathon preparation was done. A big red ribbon marked the finish line. As starting time approached, the press was slowly moving into place, and the refreshment table was already ladened with goodies.

By six-thirty, all the Sticks were awake and back at the Factory, except for Mr. Shadow who was still on Buggles's watch and Calvin who always had trouble with early mornings. Mr. Gamble paced around the rec room trying to figure out how to get his son back.

"But what about the food table?" Candle pleaded for the third time that morning. "The rats warned Romeo..."

"I don't care about the rats!" blared Mr. Gamble. "I'm trying to save my son!"

"But...but," Candle tried. But it was no use. Mr. Gamble wouldn't listen. In fact, nobody would. Not even Mr. Sox.

"We have to focus on what we know, child," he told Candle earlier that morning. "We know where Romeo is, and we know who's got him. Understand?"

But she didn't understand. Didn't they realize what monstrous calamity lay ahead if that food wasn't delivered to the starving rats? Hadn't they listened to a single word Romeo had told them?

It was almost seven o'clock, and Candle knew there was very little time left. Food by seven, the rats warned Romeo. Or else the kid gets it! Candle walked slowly behind the others, thinking to herself. Forming her own plan.

When Calvin awoke, he went immediately back to Buggles's apartment to check in with Mr. Shadow, even though he was terrified at the thought of going. He had had a terrible nightmare that he was trapped inside the apartment, starving and alone. Buggles was above him holding a chicken and wearing a dog collar. It was really weird.

Finally reaching the building, Calvin could see Mr. Shadow at his post on the large branch. I hope he's got some good news, Calvin thought. But as he got closer, he realized, uh-oh...Shadow had fallen asleep!

Chapter Ten

The leaves shivered from Shadow's snoring, and drool dripped down to the street. Calvin grabbed the closest twig he could find and smacked Mr. Shadow on the noggin. "Wake up! Wake up, you lazy bones!" Calvin roared. "What the heck happened?"

Mr. Shadow lifted his heavy lids and broke a thin strand of drool that was still connected to the branch. "Wha...," he mumbled, smacking his gooey lips together. "Calvin, what are you doing here? Where am I?"

Calvin stared at him with great disappointment. "How could you fall asleep?"

"Oh, my!" Mr. Shadow cried, snapping back into reality. "Did I fall asleep? Could I have...." Just then, Mr. Shadow tried to get up, but his back legs were still quite stiff and asleep. They just hadn't been the same since he broke them so badly on the island.

Finally standing, he began to wiggle and wobble on the branch until..."Oh, no!" he cried as he plummeted to the ground, crashing into awnings and vines along the way. He'd be fine. In big trouble, but fine.

Calvin knew it was now up to him. He took in a deep breath, stood up straight and tall and marched up to the window. Looking through the cigarette burned curtain, he didn't see the cardboard box. In fact, he didn't see anything. No Romeo. No Buggles. No Chip. The place was empty! Was Buggles really going to do it? Was he was really doing away with Romeo at the finish line?

"I'm too late!" Calvin cried in horror. "Come on, Shadow! Let's go!"

When everyone back at the Factory found out about Mr. Shadow sleeping on the job, they became enraged.

"How could you?" Mr. Gamble barked.

"You're supposed to be the one in charge of safety!" Fluffy cried.

Snickers didn't say anything, unless you count the expulsion of a toxic gas.

Mr. Sox paced wearily around the room. "Good job, Shadow," he said with sharp sarcasm. "Now you've set us back hours! Maybe even for good!"

Mr. Shadow sat on his bottom and stared at the floor in shame, mud dripping from the tip of his nose. "I'm sorry! I'm sorry! I'm sorry!" he wept, clenching his front paws together and throwing himself at Mr. Sox's ankles. Pathetic.

"Get off of me!" Sox shouted. "Go stand with the others."

Shadow unwrapped himself and slithered over to the group. He hated groveling in front of everybody like this, but what was he to do?

Mr. Sox took in a deep breath, something that was getting harder and harder every year. He stood in front of the other Sticks, his silver hair slick and groomed, and began. "The marathon will be starting soon. I don't know what's going

Chapter Ten

to happen today. Stay together!" he warned. "Tell any others you see to meet back here after the marathon. If all goes well, we will resume our opening ceremony festivities later in the day." He looked long and slow at each cat. "Good luck, out there! Keep an eye peeled for Buggles! And bring our Romeo back to us! Go!"

A battery of cats charged out the door in a tidal wave of colors, including poor Mr. Shadow. Snickers and Uncle Fred lingered in the dust.

Although no one had a clue what to do, they had the drive and determination to get the job done somehow. Romeo would be saved! That was that. They'd overcome other obstacles by sticking together in their lifetimes, this day would be no different.

At the starting line, the excitement had begun. Hundreds of runners from all around the city were huddled together like bees to honey. As they waited for the race of their lives to begin, they checked and rechecked their special marathon shoes, stretched and twisted each leg, and filled their bellies with cool, clear water.

Above, the heavens proved generous. Someone actually spotted a dot of sunlight in the gray smudge that stained the sky. "There it is, daddy!" little Betsy Lee cried from atop her father's square shoulders. "The sun!" But as fast as she saw it, it was gone.

On the sidelines, various bands and jugglers entertained the eager and excited crowd. Kooky

Life Four

Chapter Ten

clowns rode up and down on unicycles, fat women with bushy mustaches wrestled in mud pits, and two tiny dwarves danced in funny outfits. All were visitors from Quivers's Side Show and Pizza Stand. However, there was no pizza. Just a stand.

The Sticks took various positions around the street. Some, like Calvin and Snickers, slid back against the buildings, while Fluffy and Mr. Gamble charged to the front of the crowd. Candle stood alone under the food table near the cheese slices and warm grapes. It was almost seven o'clock. No sign of Romeo, or the rats.

As a hush fell over the crowd, Mayor Hashback took center stage. He stood on a platform raised high above the starting line framed against the city skyline, looking wider than most of the buildings. He glared at his little assistant off stage, and a microphone soon arrived.

"Boo! Hiss!" the crowd thundered. "Get off the stage!"

Mayor Hashback had never been a favorite among the people. He somehow made his way into office after Mayor Crowman's mysterious murder and had remained a disappointment ever since. He certainly wasn't doing anything to improve the city. Not unless you counted his plush, luxurious office. Hopefully, this marathon would generate some support, though not likely.

"Calm down! Calm down!" he roared, flailing his arms in the air above the podium. "Quiet!"

The crowd went silent.

172

Life Four

Clearing his throat, he began. "Welcome to the first annual city run-a-thon!"

"Yeah!!" the crowd cheered as the runners stretched in preparation.

"Thank you for coming out on this beautiful day," he said as a lone raindrop slid down the slope of his nose. "Two years ago I decided the city needed a new event! After some careful planning, and thanks to the nice folks at Salty Cat Foods and Quivers's Side Show, we are here today!" A flying tomato smacked him right in his face. His assistant raced on stage immediately with a towel. "As I was saying," he continued wiping tomato seeds from his eyes, "this marathon marks a new beginning for our city!" Suddenly everyone laughed and pointed. "...like I said, a new...." But the crowd continued. Apparently, the towel was covered in black paint used in making the signs, and black smudges had smeared all over his face. The assistant ran back on stage and handed the mayor a clean towel.

"Get on with it!" someone yelled.

"Let's go!" another shouted.

Infuriated, the mayor crumpled his notes and threw them on the ground. "When I shoot this gun into the air," he said, holding the pistol high above his head and feeling a tingling sense of power, "the race will officially begin!"

"Yeah!!"

The runners took their positions behind the ribbon. The bands stopped playing, the clowns stopped clowning, and the dwarves stopped dancing. Tension filled the air. The Sticks watched nervously, looking for anything or anyone suspicious. And then, Fluffy saw something.

"A rat! A rat!" he hollered in Mr. Gamble's ear, pointing as it lurked through the crowd, weaving suspiciously around an old woman's feet. It was no ordinary rat, that was for sure.

BANG! The gun exploded sending the river of runners on their way. So much training, so much adrenalin. They pounded down the street like beasts. Slow Henry, a fat and lazy businessman, was already trailing far behind. Too many donuts, no doubt, but one had to admire his determination.

"Whoo-hoo!!" the crowd cheered. The bands started to play again, the clowns, mustached ladies, and dwarves resumed their fiesta. Mayor Hashback lay on the platform, the loud backfire of the gun throwing him off his feet.

"Follow that rat!" Fluffy wailed, searching through the swarms of people. "Don't let him get away!"

"I don't see him!" Mr. Gamble cried sinking deeper and deeper into the masses.

The racers ran their hearts out while a sleepy Alley cat was just waking up with a throbbing headache. It was Irving. He lay directly in the path of the charging athletes.

Irving lifted his head when he felt the rumble beneath him. "Oh, no!" he screamed, suddenly seeing

Life Four

hundreds of runners heading his way. He struggled to get up, but he was too weak. In a frenzied panic, he held his paws over his face, and...

Stomp! Smush! Squish! The runners pulverized poor defenseless Irving into a flattened mess. Nobody noticed, not even Slow Henry bringing up the rear. Life seven. Gone.

Irving was finally dragged aside by one of the mustached ladies. "We can use him in our act!" she told her partner.

"A dead cat?" he said. "Are you out of your mind?"

You had to be out of your mind to be in Quivers's Side Show. It wasn't such a glamorous life after all. All those late nights. Low pay. Constant ridicule. The ugly side of show biz.

The city cops were hot on the trail of Buggles Flannigan. They found his secret hideout and quite mysteriously in it, a map of the marathon route. He had to be out there somewhere.

"What's he look like, Joe?" Sergeant Moloney asked.

"You remember, the guy in the picture!" Bob said making a scrunched up face and sticking out his belly. "The ugly one."

"With the bad teeth?"

"That's the one!"

But with so many people in the city crowding the streets, finding a notorious bank robber at a marathon was like finding a needle in a haystack, or harder. With their official radios in

Chapter Ten

hand, the cops scoured the sidewalks, checking under every hat and in every baby carriage. This was one tough assignment.

As the runners blew past, a heavy cloud of dust lingered in the air. Once it cleared, the cameras stopped snapping and the bands stopped playing again. All the excitement was on hold until the nail-biting finish.

Calvin had been watching the jolly sideshow performers like a starstruck teenager. To him they were celebs, making their way in the big time. The really, big time. The limelight. Getting a gig in the Quivers's Side Show and Pizza Stand was tough. Real tough. Calvin knew it took genuine, solid talent. I bet they're rich! he mused to himself, a titillating sensation inching down his spine. I'd give anything to be one of them. Anything!

"Gotta cig?" one of the mustached ladies asked another in a low, smoky voice.

"No, but the little guy does," she answered under the wirery strands of her stash. As the performers leapt off the stage for their long awaited break, Calvin got an idea. But he had to wait for just the right moment to make his move.

Meanwhile, the other Sticks continued to strategize.

"We've got a few hours until the race is over and all the runners cross the finish line," Mr. Gamble guesstimated. "Let's split up and meet back here."

"Got it!" everyone agreed.

Life Four

Together, Mr. Gamble and Fluffy headed down the race route as Mr. Shadow dashed back to the Factory. Calvin stayed put, and Candle wandered around alone, her soft, delicate tail waving in the wind as she slowly inched around the corner.

Clusters of spectators met the racers at various parts of the city as they zoomed past.

"Go Gene!" one fan cried out, waving a bagel in his hand.

"Get a move on, Slow Henry!" another yelled.

The harder Calvin thought about being a superstar, the more intrigued he became with the sideshow. I can out perform all those bozos put together! he cried. I'll show them! They'll see what real talent is! Quickly, he checked his sleek reflection in an old, car window. I'll be rich! Like a giddy school kid, he danced circles in the street, dreaming of the future fame he had been longing for.

Meanwhile, Mr. Shadow bolted back to the Factory as fast as his wobbly legs could carry him. Still desperately trying to restore his reputation as the wise leader of safety, he had a plan. This has got to work! It's got to!

In a flash, he flew through the Factory doors, charged across the rec room, and oops, right into Mr. Sox.

"What are you doing here?" Sox asked angrily. "You should be out helping the others!"

Shadow took in a quick, deep breath and

Chapter Ten

looked Mr. Sox in the eye. "The City Chime! I've got to try it again!"

Mr. Sox stared at him through his tiny spectacles in disbelief. "We've been through this! It won't work! Nobody knows what it.....is," he said with an unexpected drop in his voice.

"W-what's the matter, Mr. Sox?"

Sox put a paw to his chest and squeezed. "Nothing. It's...nothing." He stretched his aging back and swallowed slowly. "Please return to the others. You're being ridiculous!"

"Just one try, Mr. Sox! You never know!"

As Mr. Shadow defiantly rushed toward the rickety tower, Mr. Sox rubbed his chest again and closed his eyes.

Up! Up! Higher and higher Shadow climbed, reaching forbidden and dangerous landings of the Factory structure. Once at the Chime Tower and still powered by sheer will, Mr. Shadow leapt forward stretching out his paws. He reached for the long twine that hung from the chimes. As he flew through the air, his eyes widened. "I've got it!" he roared. "Professor Shadow is back!" And with all the hope in the world, he grabbed tightly to the rope, but just as he did disaster struck. The force of his jump flung him in circles. He swung back and forth, twirling around and around, smashing into the sides of the tower above the dark pit of nothingness below him. He struggled to stop his momentum, but the more he moved, the deeper his troubles got.

Life Four

Mr. Shadow finally slowed, but the whole ordeal left him in a tangled mess. The rope was wrapped all around his body like a mummy. He was stuck. He dangled in mid-air, all alone and far away from his desire to ring that chime.

Bait was napping quietly in the alley, exhausted from a full day of waiting for the meal that never arrived.

Back on the streets, Cheeseburger set out to find breakfast. He had long given up on Irving returning with food, let alone returning at all. I'm hungry! Cheeseburger drooled as he weaved through the thinning crowds looking for a tasty tuna sandwich or a nibble of ham. There's got to be something around here somewhere, Cheeseburger moaned to himself, growing dizzy from hunger. Don't forget, he had enough blubber on him to burn for a couple of lifetimes, but hunger was another story. A long, never-ending story.

It finally looked as though Cheeseburger's needs would be satisfied. Up ahead, he saw the hazy image of something interesting. Food! Dat's gotta be food! he slobbered, swaggering closer. Could I be lucky enough to find a dead mousy? Is it possible? Just a few feet away, an incredible stench slithered up his crusty nostrils. Cheeseburger stuck his paw into the mushy meal and... "Horse poop!" he shrieked out loud shaking his dirty paw. "Get it off! Get it off me!" Like a bandit, he flew down the street and around a sharp corner, right into the clutches of The Pound!

179

Chapter Ten

"I got one!" Billy the Pound guy shouted. "The dummy come right to me!"

"Stupid cat," his partner snickered.

All Cheeseburger would remember next were the interior walls of the infamous gray van.

Calvin had performed a myriad of numbers on the sideshow players, but nothing seemed to spark their attention. Not his impeccable dance routines, not his perfect leaps and jumps, nor did his famous dramatic death scene even manage to remotely turn the head of a single sideshow performer. I've got to get them to hire me, he thought, desperate to get noticed.

In a bolder move, Calvin marched right up to the director. He planted himself in front of him, cleared his throat and began to sing his heart out with unbridled confidence.

"That cat's in heat!" the fat lady cried, waving a greasy turkey leg in the air. "Throw some water at him. That'll shut him up!"

Calvin paid no attention to their lack of enthusiasm and sang even louder. This time they'd love him for sure.

"Somebody stop that awful racket!" the fat lady cried again, pressing the turkey leg against her ear to ward off the noise.

Calvin continued his finest choreography, the very stuff that landed him the Gritty Kitty ad campaign. A shuffle here, step-toe-step there. But it was no use.

SPLASH!! A huge bucket of ice-cold water

Life Four

came pouring down on poor Calvin, drenching him to the bone. Stunned silent in an agonizing chill, he dashed around the corner, shivering and humiliated. He could hear all the sideshow people laughing and mocking him. He felt like a fool. As he rung the water from his tail, he wondered, Why do I even bother? Big breaks only come once. With an ache in his heart, Calvin splashed onto the sidewalk and wallowed.

As the mayhem continued, Mr. Gamble and Fluffy scoured the alleyways. Always using his smarts, Mr. Gamble poked his head in first looking for signs of danger. He was an ex-Alley, after all, and knew what to look for. No matter how much training a Stick had, they could never match an Alley's natural instincts. "Coast's clear," he shouted to Fluffy from alley to alley. "Come on in!" Mr. Gamble's voice echoed from the darkness.

After clearing a dozen alleyways, nothing had been found. Hope had taken the first train out of town.

Only a few miles into the race, the marathon crews were busily preparing for the finish. Everything had to be ready for the winner. The cones were set, the bandstands put in place, and the long red ribbon waved gently in the wind awaiting the swipe of the first place winner. Somewhere around the corner, Buggles Flannigan was getting ready for his own celebration.

Chapter Eleven

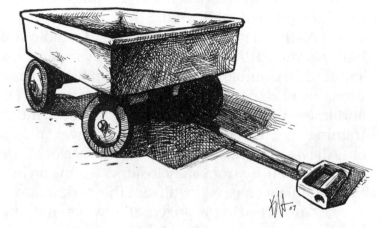

As the hours passed, the runners grew more and more weary. They puffed and coughed their lungs into rare positions, their muscles tightened in all the wrong places, and their feet blistered and swelled. But despite all the strain, they were determined. Pounding out those last few miles on the hot, tar streets, swirly visions of lemonade, ice cream, and bathtubs danced in their heads. Covered in a salty layer of sweat, they gave it all they had. Push! Push! Push! Almost there! For some it was fulfilling a life long dream, for others a walk in the park. And then there was Slow Henry.

Life Four

A losing hand at poker put him at the starting line on a dare, a game he'd never play again.

Calvin wandered closer to the finish line. Still tingling with anger over his impromptu audition, he hadn't even noticed the commotion mounting around him. Excitement filled the air as the singers, dancers, and acrobats bounced their way back out to entertain the masses. Oh, the show people are back, he thought. He turned away from the performers and headed into the crowd. Big deal. Who cares anyway?

Calvin pranced to the street corner keeping a low profile, his tail tucked tightly between his legs. Though he was nervous just being around all those cheering, screaming people, the excitement of the day drew him in like a magnet. As he inched his way closer and closer, Calvin squinted his eyes to see more of the big finish and maybe even spot Romeo in the process. Then at least he'd feel appreciated again. Just as he was about to get what he thought would be a direct view into the crowd, a little boy in an old red wagon came rolling past with his father.

"Daddy! Daddy! A kitty!" he squealed, grabbing one of Calvin's pointy ears.

The father reluctantly glanced back. "Oh, leave him alone," he insisted. "Uncle Marty will be coming along any minute. Don't you want to see him cross the finish line?"

But the small boy had other plans. Now grabbing Calvin's collar, he yanked as hard as he could flinging Calvin into his wagon. Calvin landed with a thud on the hard red metal as he suddenly felt the wagon jerk forward and zoom off. The boy's father was running down the sidewalk, the wagon clamoring behind. They were flying.

"Wahoo!" the little boy hollered. "Go faster, daddy! Go faster!"

The harder Calvin held onto the sides, the faster the wagon seemed to go, bouncing up and down over cracks and bumps, rocking on its rickety wheels. As they raced through the throng, Calvin suddenly caught the hazy glimpse of something alarming.

"Meow!" he wailed as the wagon began to slow near the big finish. That's Buggles! I see Buggles! When the wagon stopped, Calvin got a good look at Buggles hiding behind a large truck. Calvin's eyes filled with rage, and he gnawed on his bottom lip.

"Here they come! Here they come!" cried an old man from his apartment window. "I see them! They're coming!"

As the bands played and the dwarves danced, the anxious crowd turned their heads and stared off in the distance.

"He's right!" someone shouted with a hot dog hanging like a cigar. "The old man's right!"

Everyone pointed. The mayor got back on the podium, not that anybody cared, as the announcer grabbed the mike. "Ladies and gentlemen, two runners are coming down the stretch! This is it! I see them!" Two shapes came storming forward like a couple of dusty race horses. Every eye was glued. But Calvin paid no attention. He stared in Buggles's direction. Was it really him? Calvin looked harder with trembling fear and seething rage all rolled up together.

Where'd he go? Where'd he go? Calvin wondered, squinting his eyes as tightly as he could. Darn! He's gone! Calvin could still see the truck, but Buggles had split. A gnawing feeling in the pit of his stomach told him not to look away.

"Here come the runners!" the little boy roared, shaking Calvin like a rag doll. All that jostling ravaged his view. Calvin tried to swat, but the boy held on with such a tight grip, it was impossible. There was nothing he could do but wait.

The marathon winners were moments away from the red victory ribbon. Calvin was finally freed from the kid's torturous clutches and able to get a good look up and down the street. In broad daylight Buggles was slinking past Steve's Sausage-n-Coffee House in long suspicious steps toward the finish line. Calvin tried to motion some cops, but they were busy watching the race like everybody else.

Calvin looked harder at Buggles. Under his dirty, brown trench coat it appeared as though he was hiding something. Could that be...? A sudden gust of wind flung Buggles's coat wide-open revealing Romeo! He was smushed under Buggles's right arm. Under his left were two glowing red sticks of dynamite! Calvin's whiskers shot up like knives.

Calvin could see Romeo struggling and squirming, giving Buggles a hard time. Buggles used his hand to stuff Romeo deeper into his coat. "Romeo!" Calvin shouted. "Romeo! Run! Run!" He stood up quick and tall in the wagon.

"He's gonna do it, Romeo!" Calvin hissed from the red wagon. "Buggles is really gonna do it!"

But there was no way Romeo would ever hear Calvin's cries over the cheering crowd. In sheer horror, Calvin shut his eyes, bit his tongue, and waited for a big boom. Too bad, for he didn't see Romeo bolt out the bottom of the trench coat and disappear.

Buggles was frantic and out of control. His face scrunched up, and he stomped his foot like a dinosaur. With the dynamite still tucked away under his arm, Buggles raced off to catch Romeo once again. But first he'd have to find him.

"Where'd you go, you varmint?" Buggles exploded. Calvin opened his eyes and immediately saw Buggles zigzagging through the people.

"Watch it, buddy!" one angry spectator shouted. "That was my foot!"

Buggles hurried on as he searched for Romeo. His plan would not fail! From the safety of the cold red wagon, Calvin was pumped with a newfound energy. He knew from Buggles's panic-stricken face, Romeo had gotten away. *I must get to the others*, he thought. *They've got to know! They've got to know!*

When Calvin looked out into the crowd to make his own escape, he suddenly saw what appeared to be a black tornado whirling in unexpectedly. A nervous lump grew in his throat. He looked closer. Could it be? Rats! Hundreds of rats! Calvin knew at that instant Romeo had been telling the truth! The throng of rats rumbled up the block exposing a wave of savage teeth and beady eyes bubbling with anger. They were out for blood!

"Number 444 is the winner!" the mayor announced as the sweaty runner exploded through the red ribbon. "Runner Number 26 coming in second!" Wearing proud expressions, the two athletes had flown over the finish line with a final surge of adrenalin. They threw themselves to the hard pavement as the sweat sprayed from their bodies.

Calvin crouched lower in the wagon as the killer rats hurricaned closer and closer. He could feel the pounding of their claws rattling the street, and almost smell their foulness. They had yet to be spotted by the spectators. What a moment that would be.

Suddenly, it seemed as though the rats were shouting. No, they were actually chanting something! Calvin perked up his ear and struggled to listen while still searching for Romeo and Buggles. It was far too much for him to handle.

Chapter Eleven

Among the sounds of elation and joy belching from the crowd, Calvin slowly began to make out what the rats were saying. "Where's our food? Where's our food? Where's our food?" they roared over and over again like a bunch of starving prisoners. Of course, the people would never hear more than a squeak.

"Look, daddy!" the little boy shouted seeing more runners charging up the race path. "Uncle Marty! I see Uncle Marty!"

The wagon suddenly jerked toward Uncle Marty, but not before Calvin made a daring leap over the edge. In a fraction of a second he was mid-air. He caught sight of the rats crashing into the crowd through his right eye and saw Buggles's head with his left.

"Eeek!" the crowd wailed, rats zooming all around them. "Rats! Rats!" On their feet, through their legs, knocking them this way and that, the rats ravaged the festivities terrifying everyone unmercifully.

"Where's our food?" they continued to chant as they destroyed the decorations, tormented the performers, and trampled the runners. From the bandstand, the mayor took a nosedive into his convertible car and quickly raised the top. The announcer ran in dizzying circles with nowhere to hide from the invasion. His microphone fell into the crowd, pummeling a woman as two rats tangled in her hair. As she frantically tried to knock them off, the mike rolled away, amplifying the petrified screams and cries as it swam through the mob.

"Help! Help!" echoed from every corner of the city. "Help us!"

Back at the Factory, Mr. Sox shot up straight as the sound of the cries reached the rec room. *What's going on?* he wondered, hobbling over to the front entrance. He dashed outside and waited.

Calvin fell into the crowd with a thud, landing right in a fresh puddle of hot chocolate. "Youch!" he cried. Quickly shaking himself off, he knew he had to warn the other Sticks about the rats. There was no way he could handle this on his own.

Calvin tore through the frightened mass of people, keeping a watchful eye out for Romeo and other Sticks. As he raced through the herd to get away from the horror, he chanted a warning of his own. "The rats are coming! The rats are coming!" he called, charging like a hero through the city streets. "The rats are coming! The rats are coming!" Every animal in sight dashed for home, locking themselves and their families in, far from harm's way. With dramatic flare, Calvin galloped all the way to the Factory warning everyone of the catastrophe heading their way, not knowing if anyone heard his desperate cries.

Rats or no rats, Buggles continued his search for Romeo. "I know you're out there somewhere, ya stupid kitty!" he thundered over the crowd, rummaging around like a junkyard dog. "Nobody gets away from me!" Then, in a sudden flash,

Chapter Eleven

Buggles caught a glimpse of Romeo's tail. He was far down the street making a desperate escape. With his dynamite still secure, Buggles dashed forward. "I've got you now!" he growled, foam erupting from his evil grin. With the cat in reach, Buggles leapt forward as Romeo let out a piercing scream.

"Ahhh!"

Airborne, Buggles reached out to snatch Romeo, but as he fell to the ground, he collided into a passing cop. They tumbled to the pavement with a loud thud, the cop on top of the infamous criminal.

"Buggles Flannigan!" the cop exploded. "I'd know your face anywhere! We've been looking for you!"

Buggles scrambled up and quickly grabbed his matches that had fallen from his pocket. The cop grabbed Buggles by the shoulder and pulled him back. Crazed, Buggles lashed forward and prepared himself once again to grab Romeo and carry out his stupid plan, but Romeo was too far away. "Get back here, you blasted cat!" Buggles screamed, kicking his feet and pulling his hair. "I'll get you!"

"Buggles, you're coming with me!" the cop shrieked.

"Not if I can help it!" With a burst of strength, Buggles ripped himself from the cop's clutches and dashed back into the street.

"Come back here, Flannigan!" the cop yelled

Life Four

trying simultaneously to radio his partner. His hands were shaking so furiously and sweating so profusely, the radio kept popping out of his grip and falling to the ground.

Buggles ran like the wind leaving the cop in the dust. Once in the clear, he stepped out of the crowd and looked every which way. "There you are!" he cried, spotting Romeo sneaking away. "Get back here! You'll never get away from me! Never!"

Buggles chased Romeo all the way to the Factory, the rats charging from behind, the cop pulling up the rear.

Romeo sprung into the Factory whipping right past Mr. Sox. "Oh, my! Romeo!" he roared. "Where have you been?" Suddenly, Calvin came barreling through.

"The rats are coming! The rats are coming!" he cried before bolting right back out the door to warn others still nearby.

"What?" Mr. Sox yelled. At that second, he looked up and saw the swarm of beastly rodents. "Oh, heavens!" he screamed. As fast as his old body would carry him, Mr. Sox scurried across the street and hid under a torn awning. His heart was pounding faster than it could handle.

Buggles had seen Romeo run into the Factory. He watched as the rats stormed in just moments after. Buggles looked back and saw the cop and his partner approaching fast. With only a fraction of a second to react, Buggles knew there was only one thing to do. He reached for his matches.

Chapter Twelve

"One! Two! Three! Go!" Buggles roared as his ignited dynamite soared through the Factory door. Tiny sparks crackled in the air.

"Duck!" the cops yelled, jumping into a nearby bush. They fell to the ground covering their heads for protection.

Across the street, Mr. Sox watched the horrifying events. "Nooo!" he roared.

In a flash, a massive BOOM exploded throughout the Factory. Shards of glass shot out of the broken windows, splintered wooden beams crumbled into dust, and flames engulfed the inside. The force of the explosion threw Buggles ten feet into the air, crashing him down hard against the pavement

The dynamite wasn't strong enough to bring down the entire Factory, but a raging fire threatened to finish the job. Buggles watched with an evil glow as his bruised body throbbed. But he didn't care. He got his cat. "My work here is finished," he said wickedly.

"Fire! Fire!" hollered the cop into his radio. "Get a fire truck to the old umbrella factory immediately!"

Inside the melting mess, the rats scrambled for the exit. "This way!" Hog shouted to his throng of followers.

Like a wave, the murderous rats streamed outside, some smoldering from the hot flames. The ones who escaped were lucky. Others were left inside, trapped. Somehow Irving had found himself at the Factory, looking for a little peace and quiet before continuing his search for food. Instead, life eight gone.

The handful of Sticks who had been in the library came pouring out the front door after the big boom.

"What's happening?" Fluffy cried.

"Follow me! Now!" Mr. Sox insisted, gallantly trying to lead everyone across the street to safety. Rather than follow his lead, the Sticks ran in a panic into the frenzied marathon mob, crashing through the crowd, past the bandstand, and head first into some oncoming runners. With a sudden pack of crazed felines weaving between their legs, the runners tripped and fell, tumbling to the ground in a messy, tangled disaster. Water jugs spilled, medals snapped from their ribbons as the panicked Sticks tore through the mob.

Slow Henry didn't even make it to the finish line. Two Sticks knocked him over. He hit his head and passed out cold three inches away from his victory photo. Other runners trampled over him as they passed by. Henry would have bruises resembling shoe imprints for days.

As the chaos grew around them, the crowd became wilder. They ran in every direction trying hopelessly to head for home. But with too many frightened people charging in too many directions, home became an impossible journey. The side show performers packed their bags and headed for the train station. They had enough of this city.

Finally gathering their senses, Fluffy, Mr. Gamble, MayBell, and some of the others zoomed back to the Factory. In the distance, they could see the dark, gray smoke cloud hovering over the building.

"What's going on?" MayBell cried, her pretty body covered in soot.

"I don't know, baby!" Twinkle Toes answered back. "Let's move on!"

As they ran back, one thought remained on Mr. Gamble's mind. "Where is Romeo?" he cried out loud. "Hurry! Hurry!"

As they approached the Factory, the thick,

belching smoke was growing heavier and heavier. Everyone erupted into fits of uncontrolled coughing. Mr. Sox was standing outside showing the beginning signs of trauma. He shook and quivered in dead silence.

"Have you seen Romeo?" Mr. Gamble asked feeling the blazing heat burn his nose. "Where's Romeo?"

But Mr. Sox didn't answer. He clutched his chest and watched his beautiful Factory slowly burn through his itchy eyes.

Just before the building became completely engulfed, another flood of rats came bursting out of it and into the street, freed from beneath a fallen beam. They were coughing and choking and gasping for air. Scarier than ever, they were disfigured from the flames. Their fur singed and their exposed skin bubbled from the increasing temperatures. And then...

"Romeo! Romeo!" MayBell cried at the top of her lungs as she stared through the fiery mess toward the front door.

Everyone turned their weary heads, and sure enough, through all the burnt rats and thick smoke, Romeo came stumbling forward. An almost drunk look came over his steaming face.

"Queen Elizabeth? Mom?" Romeo babbled, staring wide eyed into space.

"He's delirious!" Mr. Gamble announced. "We need to snap him out of it!"

But Romeo wasn't just delirious. He looked

Chapter Twelve

up with a funny smile, then fell to the ground. Dead. It was over.

Unfortunately, nobody had time to react. They were still surrounded by those rats! Big, scorched rats! "Everybody, spread out!" Mr. Gamble cried. He tried to get to Romeo, but in all the chaos, it was impossible.

The rats were moving forward, their faces melted and angry. Hog stepped forward. "We had a little deal with your dead friend over there!" he yelled. "Where's our food?"

All the rats began to chant again. "Where's our food? Where's our food?" as the Sticks trembled with fear.

"It seems we have some unfinished business to take care of," Hog snapped. "I guess we need..."

Suddenly, out of nowhere a grungy, old taxi screeched forward coming to an abrupt stop. Everyone's head immediately turned. The cab door opened as if by itself.

"Here's your blasted food!" Candle screamed, pelting Hog with a cheese Danish. It splattered in his ears. "Eat it! Eat it all!" While everyone had been searching earlier, Candle found Romeo's taxi and took it upon herself to retrieve the food. The driver helped. Candle noticed his purple, glowing watch. In another stroke of luck, she spotted Calvin as he was racing by.

From behind Candle, Calvin hopped out of the taxi holding a large tray of deli meat in his paws. They instantly began whipping the food at all the rats.

"Oh, yeah?" Hog cried, running up to the cab. "Take this! And this!" From the ground he scooped up a ball of potato salad and flipped it in Candle's direction.

Pretty soon, all the Sticks and rats erupted into a massive food fight. Uncle Fred gobbled down some bologna when he thought no one was looking.

"Eat this, rats!" Calvin hollered at the top of his lungs.

As the food fight ensued, Mr. Sox became comatose in the hot glow of his burning Factory as it crumbled into dust. In one final flop, it was over. A lone party streamer floated from above. All who were there to witness the horrible disaster would be forever haunted by those final moments. Their school, their beautiful school, had been destroyed. All that was left was a pile of rubble and an empty can of blue paint. A thick cloud of ash swirled overhead before drifting into the sky and out of sight forever.

As the dust and smoke cleared and everyone hacked the muck from their lungs, something startling came to Mr. Gamble's attention. Romeo was gone. "Hog! Where's my boy?" Mr. Gamble erupted in anger, seeing the rats sneaking away. "Where's Romeo's body?"

MayBell pointed to where Romeo had fallen, but noticed immediately he had disappeared. It

Chapter Twelve

took a moment for the other Sticks to realize what was happening. They instantly filled with fright and knew his body had been taken.

The rats were far down the street by now, all except for Hog who lingered behind defiantly. "You won't be needing him any longer, or that friend of his either," Hog said with surprising calmness. "They're with us now. Don't bother looking."

"What? What are you talking about?" Mr. Gamble roared. "What friend? Tell me where they are! Get back here!"

And then Sox noticed. Shadow was missing, too. But it was too late to do anything about it. Hog and the rats had disappeared into the crowd and out of sight. Mr. Gamble collapsed to the ground in despair.

Mr. Sox looked down at him. Gamble's face had gone pale under his fur. "I know where they're taking them," Sox said.

"Where? Where?" Mr. Gamble whined in an emotionally weakened state.

"To the four corners. I'm sure of it." Mr. Sox answered as he sat down in the glow of the fire. "That's where they do their dirty work. I'm sorry. I don't know what to do."

Meanwhile, a few blocks away, Bait settled himself into his alley, still waiting for a meal. Cheeseburger finally came stumbling up. His fur was a mess, what fur he had left. His funny, twisted ear rattled back and forth, and his nostrils flared as wide as could be. "Don't ask!" he said

Chapter Twelve

to Bait. "You don't wanna know what kinda day I've been having." A few seconds later, another cat came stumbling through the alley toward them.

"Finally!" Bait sighed, his stomach growling. "There you are! Where's my breakfast?"

Irving wobbled on his four paws. "I made it. I made it," he mumbled, a peace beaming from his eyes. "Sleep." His eyes swirled hypnotically as he stared at his comfy bed. It was a glorious sight. Irving took a small step and...bang! A large chunk of scorched wood exploded out of the Factory fire landing right on Irving's head. Flop! He fell flat on his face. Dead. Nine times. This time for good.

"So much for that guy," Cheeseburger said without an ounce of emotion.

"Yeah," Bait added. "I never liked him anyway. What a weirdo."

"Now we can see what he'd hidin' in that purse of his," Cheeseburger nudged. "Come on, open it up!"

With heavy anticipation, Bait cracked open the briefcase with a jagged brick and opened it carefully. "Now we'll see what that little rodent was hidin' from us!"

Bait and Cheeseburger stared inside. "What the?" Cheeseburger said.

"I can't believes it!" Bait snarled. "After all that he had a loada tuna all along?"

Apparently, Irving's case was packed with a hearty supply of canned cat food. Why he chose never to share his secret stash would always remain a mystery. Thus, with empty bellies and drooling tongues, Bait and Cheeseburger would enjoy a feast like no other, licking their paws clean as Irving lay dead and cold. As a souvenir of this wondrous event, Bait kept Irving's silk, paisley pants tucked away and out of sight.

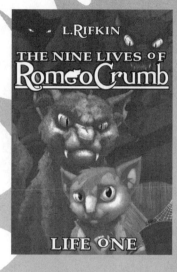

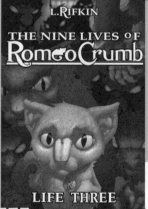

LIFE FIVE

2008

Stratford Road Press, Ltd.